The Ten Creepiest Creatures in America

Allan Zullo

D0839384

ACKNOWLEDGMENTS

I wish to thank the following people, libraries and newspapers who assisted me in the research of this book:

Carla Chadick; Alex Early, Fort Worth (Texas) Public Library; Ruth Evans, *Texarkana* (Texas) *Gazette*; Kathleen Gruver, Trenton (New Jersey) Public Library; Ila B. Lacy, Jackson County (Arkansas) Library; Lee County (South Carolina) Public Library; Louisiana (Missouri) Public Library; John McGran; Martha Moffett; Willard Reynolds; St. Tammany Parish (Louisiana) Library; and Millie Watson, *Lee County* (South Carolina) *Observer*.

Their cooperation and efforts were greatly appreciated.

If you purchased this book without a cover, you should be aware that this book is stolen property. It was reported as "unsold and destroyed" to the publisher, and neither the author nor the publisher has received any payment for this "stripped book."

Copyright © 1997 by The Wordsellers, Inc.

Published by Troll Communications L.L.C.

Cover design by Tony Greco & Associates.
Cover illustration by Phantom Design.

All rights reserved. No part of this book may be reproduced or utilized in any form or by any means, electronic or mechanical, including photocopying, recording, or by any information storage and retrieval system, without written permission from the publisher.

Printed in the United States of America.

10 9 8 7 6 5 4 3 2 1

*To my good friend Steve Duncan,
who is such a creature of politics
that it's downright creepy.*

CONTENTS

INTRODUCTION

Do strange monsters really exist in America?

Most scientists say it's not likely. But believers point to interesting evidence such as unexplained footprints, photographs of unidentified animals, and audio tapes of unknown beastly sounds—all of which defy the understanding of current science.

Most often, the only proof we have that we share this land with creepy creatures is the thousands of sightings reported by people of all ages and backgrounds. Usually witnesses reveal what they saw to their local police or sheriff's department. This suggests they are telling the truth—at least as they see it—because most people don't make false police reports, which is a crime. However, an untold number of sightings probably are never reported to the authorities. Often witnesses won't make an official report because they are afraid they will be laughed at if they say they've seen a monster.

There is no doubt that many sightings, photos, and footprints of alleged monsters are the result of elaborate hoaxes, mistaken identity, overactive imaginations, and outright lies. Also, it's sometimes hard to separate fact from folklore or legend.

Nonbelievers claim that monsters couldn't possibly survive in a country as densely populated as the United States. But there are still vast areas of wilderness left in our country that remain virtually unexplored. These dark forests, remote mountains, deep lakes, and steamy swamps could offer plenty of room to roam for as-yet-unclassified animals. Also, the overwhelming majority of sightings take place at night, indicating that monsters—if they exist—most likely hide out during the day.

Certain mysterious creatures may not be so mysterious at all. They might be animals long thought to be extinct but which, in fact, are not. For example, scientists believed a large fish called a coelacanth had been extinct for millions of years—until a fisherman caught one in the late 1930s and others like it were discovered later swimming in the Indian Ocean.

Still, the majority of scientists seriously doubt that any unidentified creature roams America. These experts won't change their minds until they see the proof with their own eyes. And the only proof they will accept is a monster itself—dead or alive.

So, do creepy creatures really exist in America? After reading in this book the accounts of such monsters as Lizard Man, Champ, Momo, and Whitey, you can make up your own mind.

MOTHMAN

For one unforgettable year, startled residents of West Virginia were petrified by Mothman—a bizarre flying creature that flashed terrifying eyes.

From the fall of 1966 to the fall of 1967, hundreds of horror-struck witnesses reported seeing a manlike monster with huge bat wings. Most everyone gave similar descriptions of the beast: It was about seven feet (2.1 m) tall and brownish gray. It had a small head resting on broad shoulders, two bright red eyes, legs but no arms, and ten-foot (3-m) wings that folded against its back when not in use. Although its wings didn't flap, the creature could fly straight up like a helicopter or zoom through the air at speeds of up to one hundred miles (160 km) an hour.

Most of the sightings took place within a one hundred-square-mile (250-square-km) area of Charleston, the state's capital.

The series of encounters began on November 12, 1966. Five grave diggers near Clendenin, West Virginia, claimed they observed a brown, manlike monster with wings gliding low over their heads before it disappeared into nearby trees.

Nobody took them seriously—until witnesses over the next several weeks reported they saw the same creature.

Three days after the grave diggers' sighting, on November 15, building contractor Newell Partridge spotted the beast outside his home in Salem, one hundred miles (160 km) from Clendenin. He was watching television with his wife when the screen blanked out.

"A fine herringbone pattern appeared on the tube," he told investigator Gray Barker, "and at the same time the set started to make a loud whining noise."

Meanwhile, Partridge heard his dog Bandit howling outside, so he picked up a flashlight and went to investigate. Bandit was facing the hay barn, barking and howling at something. When Partridge shined the light in that direction, he saw a manlike beast with two red eyes that looked like large bicycle reflectors. The sight sent chills down Partridge's spine. Bandit then snarled and charged the creature.

Partridge ran back inside for a gun. When he returned, Bandit had disappeared and so had the mysterious monster.

An hour later, at about eleven thirty P.M., the same creature was seen about one hundred miles (160 km) southwest of Salem near Point Pleasant, West Virginia.

Two married couples—Roger and Linda Scarberry and Steve and Mary Mallette—were driving through an abandoned World War II ammunition dump known as the TNT Area. The site consisted of several hundred acres of woods and open fields filled with large concrete domes that had stored dangerous explosives during the war. It also contained a deserted power plant. Next to the area was a 2,500-acre (1,000-hectare) animal preserve.

As the couples drove past the empty plant in the Scarberrys' car, they saw a weird figure standing beside the road staring at them.

"It was shaped like a man, but bigger," Scarberry told reporters later. "Maybe six and a half or seven feet [2 or

10

2.1 m] tall. And it had big wings folded against its back.

"For a minute we could only stare at it. Then it just turned and sort of shuffled toward the open door of the old power plant. We didn't wait around."

"It was those eyes that got us," said Linda. "It had two big red eyes, like automobile reflectors."

Not knowing what it was or what harm it could do to them, the couples tried to flee from the creature. Roger, who was driving, floored the accelerator of his car and streaked down the highway at about one hundred miles (160 km) an hour. They thought they had left the beast behind. They were wrong.

To their shock, they discovered that the creature was *flying* beside them low over the ground, its wings spread out to about ten feet (3 m). All four later claimed that the monster effortlessly kept pace with the car even though its wings were not flapping.

"I could hear it making a sound," recalled Mary Mallette. "It squeaked like a big mouse."

The beast followed their car for about seven miles (11 km), before flying off into the night at the city limits. The panic-stricken couples headed straight to the Mason County sheriff's department and reported their encounter to Deputy Millard Halstead. Although he found their story hard to believe, he knew they weren't the kind of people to make up tales.

Despite their fear, the couples agreed to return to the TNT Area with the deputy. As he parked his squad car next to the old power plant, the police radio began sending out an odd sound, like a record album played at high speed. After a search of the area, Halstead failed to find any evidence of the creature.

The next day, Sheriff George Johnson called a press conference to discuss the strange flying beast. After learning of its description, a local editor named the creature Mothman after a villain on the *Batman* TV series that was popular at the time.

Sheriff Johnson wondered if anyone else would report a Mothman sighting. He didn't have to wait long.

That night, at about nine, Mr. and Mrs. Raymond Wamsley and Mrs. Marcella Bennett and her two-year-old daughter Tina visited the Ralph Thomas family, who lived near the TNT Area. As the four got out of the car, they spotted the creature only a few yards away lying in the grass.

"It rose up slowly from the ground," Mrs. Bennett recalled. "A big gray thing. Bigger than a man, with terrible glowing eyes."

Startled beyond belief, Mrs. Bennett, who had been carrying Tina in her arms, dropped the little girl. The mother was so horrified that she stood frozen, unable to reach for her daughter.

"It was as if the thing had Marcella in some kind of trance," Wamsley later told the press. "She couldn't move."

Wamsley rushed over to help Mrs. Bennett. He scooped up Tina and ushered Marcella and his wife into the house. They bolted the door, crouched behind the furniture, and screamed in terror. By now, the bizarre beast had shuffled onto the porch and was peering into the windows. Wamsley frantically called the police, but by the time help arrived, the creature had left.

As eyewitness accounts of Mothman appeared in area newspapers and on TV and radio, the TNT Area bustled with activity. People traveled for hundreds of miles, hoping to catch a glimpse of the monster. Long lines of cars slowly circled the power plant. TV crews and out-of-state reporters gathered at the site. Hunters gripping shotguns and rifles poked into every bush. Night after night, hundreds of men, women, and children sat quietly in the cold. Watching. Waiting. Wanting to see Mothman.

12

But those who saw the creature vowed they never wanted to see it again.

Meanwhile, reports of sightings of the flying beast were coming in from all over western West Virginia.

On November 20, a Point Pleasant businessman claimed he encountered Mothman on his front lawn. After stepping outside to quiet his barking dog, the man unexpectedly faced a seven-foot (2.1-m) winged creature with "flaming eyes." The stunned man stood still for several minutes, unaware of how much time had passed. When the monster finally flew off, the man staggered back into his house. He was so pale and shaken that his wife feared he was suffering a heart attack.

The next night, a frightened Charleston resident phoned police that a "bat-man" was sitting on the roof of the house of his next door neighbor. "It looks like a man," said the caller. "It's about six feet [1.9 m] tall and has a wingspread of six or eight feet [1.9 m or 2.4 m]. It has great big eyes." He said it flew "straight up, just like a helicopter."

Mothman boldly began appearing in the daytime. On the morning of November 25, shoe salesman Thomas Ury was driving near the TNT Area when he noticed a tall, gray, manlike figure standing in a field. "Suddenly it spread a pair of wings and took off straight up, like a helicopter," Ury later told reporters. "This thing had a wingspan every bit of ten feet [3 m].

"It veered over my convertible and began going in circles three telephone poles high. It kept flying right over my car, even though I was going about seventy-five miles [125 km] per hour.

"I never saw anything like it," added Ury, who sped straight to the sheriff's office after the creature flew away. "I was so scared, I just couldn't go to work that day.

"I've never had that feeling before—a weird kind of fear. That fear gripped you and held you. Somehow, the best way to explain it would be to say that the whole thing just wasn't right. I know that may not make sense, but that's the only way I can put into words what I felt."

The next day, Mrs. Ruth Foster of St. Albans, a suburb of Charleston, claimed that Mothman appeared in her front yard. "It was standing on the lawn beside the porch," she recalled. "It was tall with big red eyes that popped out of its face. It had a funny little face. I didn't see any beak. All I saw were those big red poppy eyes. I screamed and ran back into the house."

Around the same time in St. Albans, thirteen-year-old Sheila Cain and her sister saw Mothman standing in a junkyard. The girls later told police they screamed, and as they rushed home, the creature kept flying only a few feet above them.

The following morning, Connie Carpenter, of New Haven, a few miles north of Point Pleasant, received the shock of her life. She said she was driving home from church when she observed the beast flying straight toward her car.

"Those eyes! They were very red, and once they were fixed on me, I couldn't take my own eyes off them," she declared. "It's a wonder I didn't have a wreck."

She said the creature flew directly at her windshield, then veered off and disappeared. She said its face "was horrible—like something out of a science-fiction movie."

At the Gallipolis, Ohio, airport just across the Ohio River from Point Pleasant, five local pilots reported seeing a strange birdlike creature on the afternoon of December 4. As the winged beast glided low over the water, they mistook it for an airplane. It was about three hundred feet (90 m) up, traveling an estimated seventy miles (110 km) an hour—without flapping its wide wings.

When they realized it was something they had never seen before, one of the pilots grabbed his camera, jumped into his plane, and took off after it. But by the time the pilot was airborne, the monster had disappeared.

John Keel, well-known author and investigator of the unexplained, made five trips to West Virginia to conduct his own probe into the Mothman mystery. He learned that several witnesses had seen the creature more than once—and many of them were emotionally traumatized from the experience.

Mrs. Marcella Bennett, who encountered Mothman on November 16, did not recover fully from her terrifying experience for many months.

"And more months passed before she was able to discuss what she had seen with anyone, even her own family," wrote Keel in *The Complete Guide to Mysterious Beings.* "Her trauma was so real that she had to start seeing a doctor on a weekly basis. She was plagued by frightening dreams and believed that the monster repeatedly visited her home, a small house somewhat isolated on the outskirts of Point Pleasant."

Mrs. Bennett told Keel back then, "I know it has been here. I can feel it when it's around. And I've heard it. It makes a terrible sound that goes right through your bones. It sounds like a woman screaming."

Roger and Linda Scarberry, two of the first people to report a Mothman sighting at the TNT Area, claimed they saw or felt the presence of the creature "hundreds of times."

Linda told investigators: "It seemed like for two years it would follow us everywhere we went. It seems like it doesn't want to hurt you. It just wants to communicate with you. But you're too afraid when you see it to do anything. You think about getting away. I keep wanting to go back to find out what it is, but I don't want to see it again.

"We rented an apartment down on Thirteenth Street, and

the bedroom window was right off the roof. [Mothman] was sitting on the roof one night, looking in the window, and by then I was so used to seeing it I just pulled the blinds and went on. I felt kind of sorry for it because it gives you the feeling like it was sitting there wishing it could come in and get warm because it was cold out that night."

Virginia Thomas, who had seen Mothman in the TNT Area on the afternoon of November 2, 1967, believed the creature had eerie mental powers. "It took over my thinking, like it could pick it up and take it away from me," she told Keel. Mrs. Thomas added that when she encountered the monster, she felt paralyzed, unable either to move or to take her eyes off it. All the while, her ears kept popping.

By the end of the fall of 1967, there were no more reported encounters with Mothman. The last major sighting took place November 7, when four hunters claimed they saw a giant winged manlike creature with red eyes gliding a few feet off the ground. The witnesses were too awestruck to raise their guns.

After conducting his own investigation, Keel concluded that Mothman may have been an extraterrestrial. People throughout the region reported seeing UFOs beginning in the fall of 1966—the same time when Mothman first appeared. Keel found cases where cars passing by the TNT Area unexplainably stalled. TV sets and radios, including some new ones, burned out without cause.

In his book, Keel wrote, "Many of these [UFOs] moved at treetop level. There were also many daylight sightings of strange circular objects, particularly in the TNT Area. By the end of 1967, over one thousand UFO sightings by responsible witnesses had been recorded throughout the [area]."

Typical of the UFO witnesses was Mrs. Roy Grose, a music teacher who lived across the Ohio River, almost directly opposite the TNT Area.

16

At four forty-five A.M. on November 17, she was awakened by her dog's barking. She looked out the kitchen window and in the moonlight saw an enormous, brightly lit UFO hovering at treetop level in a nearby field. The object was circular and the size of a small house. Glowing with dazzlingly bright red and green lights, the UFO zoomed off in a zigzag motion and disappeared.

Explanations of what Mothman was ranged from a large bird known as a sand hill crane (very rare in West Virginia) to a jokester in a hang glider. Witnesses said there was no way they could mistake a bird for Mothman. Besides, they added, birds don't fly straight up like a helicopter.

A hang-gliding jokester seemed doubtful, because he couldn't fly fast or straight up.

"Mothman was ill-suited for flight," said Keel. "A creature larger than a big man, and therefore weighing in excess of two hundred pounds [90 kg], would require more than a ten-foot [3-m] wingspan to get aloft."

According to another theory, the whole thing started as a joke but got out of hand. There was so much publicity that people became convinced the story was true. Then they began to imagine seeing Mothman themselves—a classic case of "mass hysteria."

Whatever it was, Mothman was no hoax in the opinion of investigators. Unlike many other monster sightings, this one had an impressive number of cases where more than one witness saw it at the same time. Also, the witnesses were considered by authorities to be extremely reliable.

Wrote Keel, "We investigated the situation in Point Pleasant as thoroughly and as carefully as was humanly possible. But after all of our interviews and all of our experiences, we were still left with the basic, disturbing question: What is really on the loose in West Virginia?"

THE HONEY ISLAND SWAMP MONSTER

T hey say it stands seven feet (2.1 m) tall . . . weighs four hundred pounds (180 kg) . . . leaves four-toed, alligatorlike tracks in the mud . . . is covered with short, clingy gray hair . . . has a massive chest and shoulders . . . and boasts a set of razor-sharp claws that can rip flesh to shreds.

They call it the Honey Island Swamp Monster.

According to believers, there is more than one such creature. Because different-sized tracks have been discovered, some people think the beast is part of a group of beings who have survived in a dangerous place that few humans would dare to visit.

The monster supposedly lives deep in the 47,000-acre (17,000-hectare) snake-infested, moss-draped swamp that's only a short drive from New Orleans, Louisiana. In the Honey Island Swamp, sluggish waterways twist and turn through forests of huge cypress trees that shade birds, frogs, bear, deer, alligators, and wild boar.

The swamp got its name from an island in the center that centuries ago was thick with bees. The bees on the island produced honey for the Choctaw Indians who lived in the area.

During the pirate days of the 1700s and 1800s, the swamp

was a hideout for outlaws. According to local legends, millions of dollars in gold and other valuables are still hidden there.

And apparently so is the Honey Island Swamp Monster.

In the early 1970s, Frank Davis, a freelance writer who worked with the Louisiana Wildlife and Fisheries Commission, heard stories that hunters and fishermen had seen a hideous creature. But none of them would talk openly about their encounters with it because they didn't want their families and friends to make fun of them. A local publication called *Tammany* found other eyewitnesses, but they too refused to have their names published.

Then Harlan E. Ford stepped forward. He was a well-known hunter and fisherman who lived in Slidell, a town on the edge of the Honey Island Swamp.

Ford said he and a friend came face-to-face with the beast during a hunting trip in 1973 on a remote part of the swamp's Honey Island. The men were hacking their way through incredibly thick grass and brush when they finally reached a small clearing.

"That's when we saw the thing," Ford later told Davis. "It must have heard us thrashing through the brush, but it was standing with its back to us. My friend and I both stood and stared at it. Neither of us had ever seen anything like it before, and we had trouble believing our eyes.

"Then the thing turned around and looked at us. It was ugly and sinister. Sort of like something out of a horror movie. I'm sure it was at least seven feet [2.1 m] tall, and it must have weighed four hundred pounds [180 kg]. The hair on its head hung down about two feet [.7 m]. The rest of it was covered with short, dingy gray hair. Its chest and shoulders were massive. Its face was square and mean, and I could see two rows of teeth in its powerful jaws. The thing must have stood staring at us for a full minute before it went tearing off into the woods. I want you to know it scared me real bad."

Despite his fear, Ford wanted to learn more about this creature. For the next couple of weeks, the hunter returned to the area almost daily, hoping to get another look at the monster. Ford always carried a rifle on these trips, although he hoped he would never be put in a situation where he would have to shoot the beast in self-defense. But he never saw the creature again.

He did find interesting clues, however. He showed reporters a cast of the monster's tracks—strange-looking, four-toed imprints that looked like a cross between the feet of a large alligator and a big man.

"We poured plaster-of-Paris casts of the thing's tracks at the site of what we believe is its watering hole," Ford told the press. "The site is deep in the swamp, thick and overgrown, and I doubt seriously that more than a dozen men had ever been in that section of Honey Island."

Ford found many similar tracks—some slightly smaller and others slightly bigger. "There's a good chance that there is more than one Honey Island Swamp Monster," he said. "There is no way every set of prints could have been made by the same creature."

Ford told *Tammany* he knew where the beast was hanging out, but the hunter didn't want others to learn of the exact location for safety reasons. "As far as I know, the monster hasn't harmed anyone," he said. "But a little while ago, three large wild hogs were found in the area where the creature lives. Each one had its body mangled and its throat torn out. I don't want to tell curiosity-seekers the monster's whereabouts, because I'd feel responsible if the creature harmed or killed anyone."

After Ford told his story to local newspapers and a New

Orleans television station, other residents of Slidell and nearby Covington came forward to reveal their encounters with the Honey Island Monster. But these witnesses insisted on keeping their names out of the press.

Weeks after Ford observed the swamp beast, three men from Covington claimed they saw the creature. According to their published account, they had set up camp in the swamp after fishing on the Pearl River, which runs through the swamp. "We were relaxing around the fire late that night," recalled one of the campers, in Elwood Baumann's book *Monsters of North America*. "For some reason, we began to feel uneasy—and we didn't know why. Although we hadn't heard anything out of the ordinary, we had this strange sense that we were not alone. It was weird because we all felt as though someone—or something—was watching us."

One of the men picked up a flashlight and searched outside the perimeter of the campsite. About twenty yards (18 m) away, he heard a creature crashing through the brush in front of him. The man aimed his flashlight toward the sound and then gasped in astonishment. The beam of light fell on a large, hairy beast who was running upright on two legs toward the river.

The shocked man yelled for his friends, who rushed to his side. They reached the bank just in time to see the creature splash into the water and disappear into the darkness.

"We ran back to our camp and tried to figure out what to do," said one of the men. "We don't scare easily, but I admit we were scared. None of us wanted to spend the night there—not with that monster out there. We weren't too thrilled about trying to find our way out of the swamp when it's pitch black. But we felt we didn't have much choice. We gathered all of our equipment, dumped it into our boat, hopped in, and set off in the night for home."

In another unsettling encounter, a fishing guide and his client told Frank Davis that they may have accidentally hurt the creature a year earlier.

The men said they were on the Pearl River in their boat motoring slowly upstream through the swamp. Suddenly, the boat struck an object that was just below the surface. "I thought we might have hit an alligator or a big turtle," recalled the guide. "I stopped to take a look in the water. I couldn't see what we hit, but it felt like it was an animal of some kind. Then my client jumped up and down in our boat and shouted and pointed toward shore.

"It was hard to believe. We both saw this big, gray, furry creature scrambling out of the water. Once it reached the bank, it immediately raced off and disappeared into the swamp." The men's descriptions of the creature were similar to those given by other witnesses.

Davis learned of a hunter who claimed he saw the creature running through a wooded part of the swamp. "It was around dusk," said the witness. "At first I thought it was a bear, but it was on two feet and moving pretty fast. It had gray hair and was huge. I was so startled I didn't move. By the time I regained my senses, it was long gone."

A man from Slidell reported that the creature stalked him and his wife during a camping trip in the swamp in 1970. "We could hear something big stomping in the woods as we collected firewood," said the man. "All of a sudden, we got a glimpse of it. My wife screamed. This was a big, hairy monster. We got out of there in a hurry—and we're convinced he stalked us, because we could hear him walking behind us."

Davis heard from another witness who claimed he shot at the beast one evening while out fishing. "I was on Lake Borgne, close to shore, when I saw this horrible monster staring at me from behind a tree. I had my rifle with me, so I fired at him. I don't think I hit him, but I sure scared him—about as much as he scared me, I think."

Several years earlier, during one of the Pearl River's many floods, two creatures matching the description of the Honey Island Swamp Monster were sighted by a motorist who had stopped along Interstate 10 east of Slidell. The beasts were walking in a swampy area by the side of the road before they vanished into the brush, said the witness.

Other than eyewitness accounts and the plaster casts Ford made of the creature's footprints, authorities have little evidence to prove that the Honey Island Swamp Monster exists.

A zoologist from Louisiana State University examined the casts. According to a 1975 story in the *St. Bernard News,* the scientist said that the monster was most likely similar to ones reported to live in the swamps of Mississippi, Georgia, and the Florida Everglades.

"We still don't know what sort of a creature it was that made these tracks," said the scientist. "This whole business of the Honey Island Swamp Monster is a complete mystery to me. The creature could be a mutant of some sort or simply an animal we haven't discovered yet. That doesn't sound very scientific, I know, but it's the only answer I have."

Ford said that several other scientists from Louisiana colleges examined the footprint casts. But these experts couldn't make any positive identification of what—or who—made the tracks. Officials have yet to prove that the creature is a hoax.

Nonbelievers argue that if the swamp monster does live on Honey Island, it certainly would have been spotted years ago. But believers say that the creature is nocturnal, meaning that it roams around only at night, so it's unlikely anyone would ever see one—especially in an area as remote as Honey

Island. Besides, its watering hole is so hidden and hard to get to that few people have ever stepped foot anywhere near it.

So what is this swamp monster? Most everyone in the area has a favorite theory. Among the most popular, the monster is believed to be:

• a mutated species of man.

• a prehistoric cousin of man who was thought to have died off but is still alive.

• a hallucination, the kind of mirage that people see when they're in the swamp too long.

• a jokester going out in the swamp at night and putting tracks in the mud with a big fake foot.

• a member of a lost Native American tribe.

• one of several mentally retarded humans abandoned by their parents in childhood in the 1940s.

• one of several mental patients who escaped from institutions in the 1960s.

Wrote local reporter Paul Serpas: "At a recent convention of the American Anthropological Association, an ancient carved stone head, representing an unknown type of animal, was displayed. The carving is remarkably similar to the descriptions generally given of the Honey Island Swamp Monster. Could it be, then, that such creatures were known hundreds, or even thousands of years ago, but have managed to go undetected by modern science?"

CHAMP

Champ is America's answer to the Loch Ness Monster. Like the famed dinosaurlike water creature in Scotland, Champ has fascinated witnesses for nearly two centuries.

Champ supposedly lives in Lake Champlain, which is 109 miles (175 km) long and eleven miles (18 km) wide and stretches along the New York–Vermont border to Quebec, Canada. As the largest body of water in the eastern United States outside the Great Lakes, Champlain is home to about eighty different kinds of fish—more than enough to feed a strange species of water monster that believers have nicknamed Champ.

Joseph Zarzynski, who has investigated and written about the creature, has cataloged more than three hundred sightings of Champ since the early 1800s. Zarzynski is founder of the Lake Champlain Phenomena Investigation, which interviews witnesses and conducts extensive visual and electronic surveillance of the lake.

Based on eyewitness accounts, this is the general description of the monster:

Champ is about fifteen to thirty feet (4.6 to 9.1 m) long and has an estimated weight of one to two tons (900 to 1,800 kg). It has dark skin, a snakelike head with two horns or ears, a mouth and teeth, and a possible ridge on its head and neck. Seen mostly during clear weather when the lake is calm, the creature has shown the ability to dive and swim at considerable speeds, sometimes with its head held high. It's quite shy and passive.

The earliest known newspaper story about the monster in Lake Champlain appeared in a newspaper called the *Plattsburgh* (New York) *Republican* on July 24, 1819. The account said that a Captain Crum spotted a creature swimming in Bulwagga Bay, New York, that was "very long and held its head more than fifteen feet [4.6 m] high."

Over the next sixty years, sailors, fishermen, and swimmers reported seeing a serpentlike creature in the waters.

According to a story in the *Whitehall* (New York) *Times* on July 9, 1873, railroad workers were laying track on the lake shore near Dresden, New York, when they "saw a head of an enormous serpent sticking out of the water and approaching them from the opposite shore." The crew stood paralyzed in fear for several moments before scattering. The creature then turned toward the open water and left.

According to the *Times*: "As he rapidly swam away, portions of his body, which seemed to be covered with bright, silver-like scales, glistened in the sun like burnished metal. From his nostrils he would occasionally spurt a stream of water above his head to an altitude of about twenty feet [6 m]. The appearance of his head was round and flat, with a hood spreading out from the lower part of it like a rubber cap often worn by mariners with a cape to keep the rain from running down the neck. His eyes were small and piercing, his mouth broad and provided with two rows of teeth, which he displayed to his beholders. As he moved off at a rate of ten miles [16 km] an hour, portions of his body appeared above the surface of the water, while his tail, which resembled that of a fish, was thrown out of the water quite often. His head was said to be twenty inches [50 cm] in diameter. A quarter mile [400 m] into the lake, the creature sank suddenly out of sight."

Whatever it was, it apparently could move on land, because days later, farmers in the area complained of missing livestock. Strange tracks and other marks in the ground indicated that an unidentified creature had dragged the animals into the lake. Meanwhile, several residents claimed they saw "bright and hideous-looking eyes" in a waterfront cave at night. A farmer said he fired at the serpent in a lakeside marsh, but the beast slipped unharmed into the water.

After more sightings and livestock kills, search parties prowled the shoreline and surrounding farms. In early August a small steamship, the *W. B. Eddy*, reportedly struck the serpent and nearly overturned near Dresden. The head and neck of the creature surfaced one hundred feet (30 m) away for a minute and then disappeared under the water.

Six years later, the *Plattsburgh Republican* reported that a group of fishermen gave a nearly identical description of a strange beast they saw near St. Albans, Vermont. "The water near the Champlain Sea Serpent lashed into foam and was thrown thirty or forty feet [6 or 9 m] high," said the account of May 17, 1879.

In 1881, the same newspaper ran a story that passengers aboard a steamboat near Swanton, Vermont, were standing on the rear deck when they spotted an enormous water creature. Although it was not swimming toward the boat and didn't appear to be a threat, Captain Warren Rockwell shot at it several times until it dived under the surface.

On August 4, 1883, the *Plattsburgh Republican* reported that Clinton County Sheriff Nathan Mooney was on board the

boat *Nellie* when he saw an "enormous snake or water serpent
. . . twenty-five to thirty-five feet [7.6 to 11 m] in length and
seven inches [18 cm] in diameter." The sheriff said its head
was about five feet [1.5 m] above the water and its neck was
curved.

During the summer of 1886, sightings were registered
almost daily from all over the lake. One man fishing near
Plattsburgh claimed to have hooked what he first thought was
an enormous fish. But when its head reared out of the water,
he and three other witnesses saw it was a huge "horrible
creature." The line snapped, and the unwanted catch
disappeared underwater.

The *Burlington* (Vermont) *Free Press* reported on July 16
that fishermen aboard the *Hattie Bell* observed a large beast
that was "fourteen feet [4.3 m] out of the water, its head
visible, showing a red tongue and eyes glowing wildly."

As sightings continued into the next year, many people
were impressed with the creature's speed in the water: "faster
than the fastest steamboats" . . . "going with great force and
speed into the wind" . . . "going at railroad speed" . . .
"moving at a pace four times the speed of any yacht."

On July 16, 1887, the *Plattsburgh Republican* reported
that a party of lakeside picnickers from Charlotte, Vermont,
were scared witless by the monster. Seventy-five feet (23 m)
long and as big around as a barrel, the serpentlike animal bore
down on the group until several women screamed. Then it
turned around and swam off.

Although virtually all witnesses reported seeing the
creature swimming in the lake, there were a few who claimed
they saw it on land.

Shortly after the picnickers' experience, this report was
published in the *Plattsburgh Morning Telegram*:

"The sea serpent . . . has left the lake and is making his

28

way overland in the direction of Lake George [in New York, about a mile from the southwestern edge of Lake Champlain]. He was seen last night about five o'clock by a farmer driving to his barn with a load of hay. Chancing to look behind him . . . he saw . . . [the creature] gliding along like a snake with its head raised about four feet [1.2 m] from the ground. . . . [It was] an immense monster anywhere from twenty-five to seventy-five feet [7.6 to 23 m] in length, with gray and black streaks, running lengthwise of its body, which was covered with scales."

Around this time near the northern edge of Lake Champlain, a St. Albans hunter claimed he observed the beast. The man was hunting ducks along the Missisquoi River, which flows out of the lake, when he came upon an "enormous serpent coiled up on the swampy shore and asleep . . . as large around as a man's thigh." As the hunter reached back to get his gun, the slight noise he made was enough to awaken the creature, which bolted toward the underbrush "making as much noise . . . as a large hound would."

On September, 26, 1889, the *Essex County* (New York) *Republican* ran a story about how a group of fishermen on the lake chased the monster near Juniper Island, Vermont. They said that the snakelike head was out of the water and that fifteen feet (4.6 m) of its body was visible. The fishermen added that the creature had "many large fins."

Three years later, on August 4, 1892, dozens of members of the American Canoe Association were terrified by a "large water serpent." Witnesses said they were paddling in the lake during their annual outing when suddenly the monster rose up in the middle of their fleet of canoes. The panic-stricken canoeists scattered in all directions, paddling for their lives. They later admitted that the beast did not attack or even threaten anyone.

Exactly seven years later, in 1899, the *Plattsburgh Republican* said a "wealthy New Yorker" saw a thirty-five-foot (11-m) serpent with an arched back, a head "like an inverted platter" and a broad flat tail raised a few feet out of the water.

Over the next forty-six years, there were very few reported sightings of the creature. But many people began seeing it again in 1945, especially near Rouses Point, New York, near the lake's Canadian border.

Mr. and Mrs. Charles Langlois claimed they were out in the lake in their rowboat when a "twenty-foot [6-m] long serpent that was as thick as a keg [barrel]" surfaced nearby. The petrified couple watched in astonishment as it swam toward them. Finally, the beast came so close to their rowboat that Charles was able to "whack it with an oar."

Days later, passengers aboard the *S.S. Ticonderoga* were on deck observing a bridge-opening ceremony when they spotted the creature poking its head out of the water.

In 1951, Mrs. Theresa Megargee claimed she saw Champ—as it was now called—three times that year off Valcour Island, New York. She said the monster was at least thirty feet (9.1 m) long. On her third sighting, Mrs. Megargee said, the water beast came too close to shore where she and her child were standing. So the mother grabbed an old rifle and shot at Champ. "At that time," she recalled, "I thought my beautiful baby might one day be a tempting *hors d'oeuvre* [appetizer] for the creature, and I was a protective young mother."

Throughout the 1950s and 1960s, Champ was usually spotted in the northern half of the lake. There were a few rare reports that the animal had temporarily beached itself.

In the spring of 1961, Thomas E. Morse claimed he saw a "thirty- to fifty-foot [9.1- to 15.3-m] long eel-like creature crawl out of the water and onto shore" near North West Bay, New York. He said it "appeared to be a monstrous eel with white teeth that raked rearward in the mouth."

In the summer of 1970, passengers aboard a ferry between Essex, New York, and Charlotte, Vermont, reported seeing Champ swimming slowly nearby.

Among the witnesses were Richard Spear and his thirteen-year-old daughter Susanne. Spear later told the *Plattsburgh Valley News* that the two of them were sitting atop the ferry enjoying the ride. Suddenly, Spear recalled, he saw the creature about ninety yards (80 m) from shore. It was "dark brownish-olive and the size and shape of a barrel in cross-section." He saw "two bumps, each rising to about three feet [1 m] above the surface and four feet [1.2 m] in length, separated by about the same distance." When his daughter looked through the binoculars, she saw its head, which reminded her of a horse's.

Another ferry witness, Anne "Happy" Marsh, later told the same newspaper that she saw "a large snakelike creature swimming with her head above water." Anne added, "I am no judge of size, but I should say she was between eighteen and twenty feet [5.5 and 6 m] long. She was black, and swimming slowly. Her head was about three feet [1 m] long, wrinkled like a raisin, with a small ridge down the back, a snake body, and was blackish-brown." Anne said she had seen the creature once before, in 1965 or 1966.

Also in the summer of 1970, passengers aboard another ferry observed Champ in the water near Burlington, Vermont.

As the lake became more crowded with boaters, sightings of Champ increased—and so did jokes from nonbelievers. Some witnesses were afraid to come forward because they didn't want to be ridiculed.

In 1971 Mrs. Robert A. Green, her mother, and a friend

stopped at a hotel overlooking the lake at Bulwagga Bay. As they gazed at the calm waters, they saw a snakelike head and three dark humps glide by. Seeking a witness outside her own little group, Mrs. Green called over the hotel bartender. He took one look and seemed stunned. Returning to the bar, he shook his head and declared, "I'll never say I saw it."

Mrs. Green told the *Baltimore Sun* that her friends back home laughed at her when she told them she had seen a "super-long thing with three humps" in the lake. Mrs. Green believed that a lot of other people had seen the monster as well, but were afraid to say so out of fear of being mocked.

Retired mine worker Walter F. Wojewodzic waited nearly ten years before he revealed publicly that he and his friend Dick Gilbo had seen Champ in Bulwagga Bay at about the same time that Mrs. Green observed it.

While duck hunting, he recalled, the men spotted three gray humps about three feet (1 m) high making a wake three hundred yards (275 m) out in the water. "The whole thing was about forty feet [12 m] long, and we couldn't even see a head," he recalled. "We watched it for about a minute and a half as it traveled a few hundred feet. Then it dived.

"The lake was as smooth as glass that day. I've fished this lake for forty-five years, and I can tell you it wasn't any kind of wave, fish, or animal I ever saw. There's something big in that lake—awfully big."

By the mid 1970s, Champ investigator Joseph Zarzynski had compiled more than 120 confirmed sightings of the creature. But there was still no proof that Champ really existed. The first piece of strong evidence came on July 5, 1977. That's when Champ was photographed.

Anthony and Sandra Mansi, a Connecticut couple who were engaged at the time, were watching Sandra's two children (from a previous marriage) wade in the lake near St. Albans.

32

Suddenly, Sandra noticed bubbles in the water about 150 feet (45 m) from shore. A huge animal with a small head, long neck, and humped back rose to the surface. As it moved its head from right to left, Sandra thought it resembled a dinosaur from a prehistoric age.

Although Sandra was awed by the bizarre sight, she had the presence of mind to snap a photograph of the water beast while Anthony helped the unknowing children to shore. Then they watched the creature for about four minutes before it disappeared under the water.

"We wondered if we should go to the police," Anthony told Zarzynski later. "But then we figured, if we walk into the police station and say, 'We just saw a monster in the water,' they'd laugh at us."

When the color film was developed, the Mansis were pleased to see how clear the picture turned out. However, "We didn't want to be called a bunch of nuts, so we just threw it in the photo album," Anthony recalled.

Zarzynski learned of the photo two years later after Sandra had shown the picture to friends at work. Zarzynski soon won the couple's trust and began an investigation.

He showed the photo to several experts, including George Zug of the Department of Vertebrate Zoology at the Smithsonian Institution's National Museum of Natural History. Zug said it bore no resemblance to any known animal in the lake or anywhere else.

B. Roy Frieden, of the University of Arizona's Optical Sciences Center, conducted a careful analysis of the photo through computer-imaging equipment. He found no evidence that the picture had been faked. The pattern of the lake's waves indicated the object had come up from under the surface. It wasn't moving along the surface, which would have been the case had it been a model being pulled by a rope.

33

Dr. Paul LeBlond, a University of British Columbia oceanographer, determined that the part of the object that was above water (supposedly the neck and head) could not be less than twenty-four feet (7 m) or more than seventy-eight feet (23 m) long.

The photo was published in the *New York Times* and *Time* magazine in 1981. "I personally consider it to be the single best piece of evidence on Champ," declared Zarzynski.

By now state and local officials started taking the creature more seriously. In 1980 the village board of trustees of Port Henry, New York, declared the nearby waters of Lake Champlain "off limits to anyone who would in any way harm, harass, or destroy the Lake Champlain Sea Monster."

A public hearing was held at Montpelier, the capital of Vermont, to support legislation to protect the creature. At the session, Sandra Mansi told lawmakers, "I just want you to know that Champ is there. Believe me, Champ is there."

The Vermont House—and later the New York Senate— passed a resolution protecting Champ "from any willful act resulting in death, injury, or harassment."

Sandra wasn't the only person to snap a picture of the creature. A series of seventeen photos supposedly of Champ was taken on July 17, 1981, near Shelburne, Vermont, by Mary Carty. She recalled, "A man came running up from the beach, yelling, 'It's Champ! It's Champ!' So I reached in the backseat of my car and I got the camera. The other people on the beach had seen a neck come out [of the water]. By the time I got down to the beach, the [monster's neck] had gone back underwater.

"I started taking pictures. The creature was moving and [everyone saw] more humps. At one time there were six humps out of the water." Mary said the creature was about thirty feet (9 m) long from head to tail. "I'm thinking it's something like a serpent, a snakelike creature."

34

A month later, on August 29, 1981, scientists from across the country met at a seminar in Shelburne to discuss the existence of Champ. Several experts said the creature could be a descendant of a prehistoric animal. They pointed out that scientists once believed a fish called the coelacanth had been extinct for seventy million years—until it was "rediscovered" in the late 1930s. Since then, others like it have been found swimming in the Indian Ocean.

Dr. Roy Mackal, professor of biology at the University of Chicago, said Champ could be a mammal called a zeuglodon, a primitive snakelike whale that supposedly died out twenty million years ago.

University of Arizona instructor J. Richard Greenwell, cofounder of the International Society of Cryptozoology (the study of unidentified animals), also had a theory. He said Champ could be a marine reptile known as a plesiosaur, which was thought to have become extinct about seventy million years ago. Champ's description is similar in size and appearance to such a prehistoric reptile.

Dr. George Zug, of the National Museum of Natural History, said he wasn't sure what it was. But he felt there was mounting evidence that some type of unidentified creature inhabited Lake Champlain.

Dr. Philip Reines, professor of mass communications at the State University of New York at Plattsburgh, declared, "I do believe in the existence of . . . unidentified animals." However, he added, it's possible that Champ may be nothing more than an oversized specimen of a known animal such as a sturgeon (a large fish) or an American eel.

Since the mid-1980s, the Lake Champlain Phenomena Investigation has been using high-tech sonar to search for Champ. The organization also relies on underwater photography and remote-controlled submarines such as those used for finding treasure in shipwrecks. Zarzynski, the group's founder, also is looking for a Champ carcass. He believes that such a carcass would prove the monster is a real animal without having to endanger a living Champ.

"The evidence of Champ's existence is scanty when compared to the wealth of eyewitness testimony and photographic and sonar evidence from Loch Ness," said Zarzynski. But he still feels there is enough "impressive data" on Champ to support the belief in its existence.

Meanwhile, Champ witnesses hope that no harm will ever come to the lake monster. Says Sandra Mansi, "We've got to do something to protect Champ. This creature is so magnificent and so wonderful that it has learned to coexist with us. Now let us learn to coexist with it."

BIGFOOT

F or nearly a century, hikers, hunters, rangers, and prospectors have reported seeing tall, hairy, two-legged creatures living deep in the thick forests of the Pacific Northwest.

These beasts are called Bigfoot (after the large tracks they make) or Sasquatch (from the Salish Indian word for "wild man" or "hairy man").

After analyzing thousands of sightings, researchers have compiled a detailed description of a typical Bigfoot: It usually grows to about seven or eight feet (2.1 or 2.4 m) in height and weighs from three hundred to one thousand pounds (140 to 450 kg). It has apelike features: flat face and nose, sloped forehead, and cone-shaped head. Bigfoot has long arms, a short neck (or no neck at all), and broad shoulders. It's covered entirely in gray-brown or reddish fur and usually has an overpowering odor. Its feet range from fourteen to twenty-two inches (36 to 56 cm) in length and five to seven inches (13 to 18 cm) in width, with three to five toes. It walks upright, unlike an ape or bear, and can run swiftly across rough territory. Its stride can reach from forty to seventy-two inches (102 to 185 cm). Bigfoot moves around mostly at night, is extremely shy, and prefers to live in dense, wooded areas and caves. It eats fruits, vegetables, and meat. It usually has been spotted alone, but sometimes has been seen with others, such as a mate or offspring.

Although the evidence is fascinating—thousands of reported sightings, large footprints, and even photographs and film footage of these beasts—there is still no solid proof that such creatures exist. Nothing short of capturing a Bigfoot will satisfy the scientific community. However, reports continue to filter in from people who claim to have seen such a being.

In the nineteenth century, residents of western Canada were well aware of stories about a race of hairy giants. But Americans didn't pay much attention to Bigfoot until the 1920s. That's when they began hearing news accounts of discoveries of large, strange footprints in the forests of Washington and Oregon.

In 1958 interest in Bigfoot soared after a well-publicized sighting. Heavy equipment operators near Willow Creek in northern California found many big footprints, apparently left by a huge two-legged creature. Plaster casts were made of the tracks for further study. A few weeks later, in late October, two men driving down a wilderness road reported seeing a hairy, two-legged beast cross in front of them and head into the trees.

Wes Sumerlin, who claimed to have observed the creature three times in the Blue Mountains of Washington, said he witnessed the shooting of a Bigfoot in 1962. Sumerlin said he was with several elk hunters when they spotted a Bigfoot in the trees. One of the hunters fired several shots at the monster, but it fled into the woods. Two days later, the injured Bigfoot was seen near a stream, stuffing leaves and pine needles into a large, bleeding wound in its stomach.

By now, campers and hikers were on the prowl for Bigfoot throughout the northwest. Among those who went searching for the creature was Roger Patterson, a onetime rodeo rider. Carrying a movie camera wherever he went, Patterson combed the woods, hoping for a glimpse of Bigfoot. After years of looking, he finally saw one—and managed to film it too.

On the afternoon of October 20, 1967, Patterson and a companion, Bob Gimlin, were riding on their horses up the partly dry Bluff Creek in the Six Rivers National Forest of northern California. The area had been the site of several Bigfoot sightings and tracks.

As Patterson and Gimlin began to cross a stream on horseback, they were stunned. There in front of them was a female Bigfoot squatting in the water. When she saw them, she stood up and walked briskly away.

Meanwhile, the horses panicked. Patterson's mount reared up and fell over sideways on the rider's right leg. As his horse staggered to its feet, Patterson grabbed the camera in the saddlebag, then jumped off to chase the creature on foot. Only twenty-eight feet (8.5 m) of film remained in the camera, and Patterson used all of it to record Bigfoot's retreat into the woods.

The footage became the most famous film of Bigfoot ever shot and created a stir among scientists. If it was a hoax, they said, it was a brilliant one. However, those who knew Patterson and Gimlin said the men were very honest.

Patterson insisted on his deathbed that the film was genuine. The film has been extensively studied by scientists. Most of them admit that it would be almost impossible to duplicate the anatomy and stride of the being in the film by using a man in a monkey suit.

Patterson, who died in 1972, and Gimlin swore the film was real. Backing up their claim was Bob Titmus, the first investigator on the scene after the sighting. Titmus found large footprints that followed the creature's route shown in the film. Titmus made casts of ten prints. He also discovered that the Bigfoot had gone up a hillside and had sat down for a while. Apparently it was watching Patterson and Gimlin, who had to run after their two spooked horses rather than continue their pursuit of the monster.

That same year, searchers added to the evidence of Bigfoot's existence. In an area of northern California's High Sierras, where a number of sightings had been reported, scientists had camped out for the night. Suddenly, they heard loud animal noises. The investigators recorded on audio tape a series of moans, whines, growls, grunts, and whistles.

Two electronics specialists later conducted an extensive analysis. They concluded that the sounds came from "more than one [creature]—one or more of which is of a larger physical size than an average human male."

Many park rangers have reported Bigfoot encounters.

While working as a National Park Service employee in 1977, Richard Seifried was hiking up the rugged slopes of Steen Mountain in Idaho. Below, from within a grove of fir trees, came a mighty roar that sounded like a giant gorilla. "Never before or since have I heard such a powerful, chesty roar," he recalled. "There is no animal I am aware of that can duplicate that sound—not even a male grizzly."

Seifried learned that a few months earlier, two men were driving home from a visit to Salmon, Idaho. They stopped at Wagonhammer Springs to get a cold drink of water. Suddenly, they screamed in terror when they noticed a gigantic apelike creature had been sitting on a boulder watching them. "The two men had confronted the animal at the mouth of the same canyon where I had heard the roaring sounds," said Seifried.

In 1978, at Crater Lake National Park in Oregon, ranger Roger Wade said he saw "a Sasquatch, upright-type animal" fifty yards (45 m) ahead of his car. The creature, who stood about six feet (1.8 m) tall, had fur the color of cinnamon. Wade later found fresh footprints that featured a middle toe longer than the others—an often-reported characteristic of Bigfoot.

In Idaho, eight hikers reported seeing a large, hairy creature walking down a hillside in the Nez Perce National Historical Park near Spalding. When they reached the hill, they found several sets of footprints indicating a stride much longer than a human's.

A series of Bigfoot sightings occurred in June 1982. Paul Freeman, a seasonal employee of the U.S. Forest Service, was walking in the Blue Mountains in the Walla Walla Ranger District of the Umatilla National Forest in northeastern Oregon. As he rounded a bend, he smelled a sickening stench. Moments later he saw what he thought was a large animal coming down a bank through thick vegetation. When the figure stepped into the clearing, Freeman froze. He stared in shock at an enormous creature—an eight-and-a-half-foot (2.6-m) tall Bigfoot—who stared back at him. For a few seconds, the two studied each other from a distance of about two hundred feet (60 m) before both became so scared that they ran in opposite directions.

Freeman, badly shaken, immediately notified his bosses. Two hours later, a group of Forest Service workers arrived at the site. They found twenty-one footprints measuring fourteen inches (36 cm) long by seven inches (18 cm) wide. They made three plaster casts and took several pictures of the tracks.

After a two-week investigation, the Forest Service said that "no determination can be made" concerning the identity of the creature Freeman claimed to have seen. The department had no further plans to look for Bigfoot.

But two days later, the Forest Service reported, Freeman

and Patrolman Bill Epoch had discovered forty new tracks in the Mill Creek Watershed on the Washington side of the border. Again, casts were made of the tracks.

Grover Krantz, a physical anthropologist at Washington State University, examined the casts from both locations. He determined that the tracks had been left by two separate creatures, each with feet about fifteen inches (38 cm) long. More intriguing, he found that the casts showed signs that the feet had dermal ridges—swirls of lines similar to fingerprints—and even sweat glands. According to Krantz, such detail could not have been faked.

The dermal ridges were fine lines about half a millimeter apart in the skin of the feet. Medical scientist Benny Kling concluded that the dermal ridge patterns were those of a highly developed, humanlike animal. But the shapes of the foot and toe were different from those of a human or an ape. Some of the ridges were worn smooth, indicating that the creature had walked barefoot for a long time.

Meanwhile, a search party from the Umatilla County Sheriff's Department, which was looking for a lost boy, followed Bigfoot tracks that went on for nearly three quarters of a mile (1.2 km). Experts were convinced this was no hoax.

"It would not be possible to fake the tracks without a helicopter," said Art Snow, who headed the search team. "We assumed Freeman was telling the truth, and we could find no evidence whatsoever" to think otherwise.

The footprints appeared real because there were no human prints around the Bigfoot tracks. The distance between each footprint suggested that whatever made them had a very long stride. Moreover, the footprints sank so deeply into the ground that researchers said they could not have come from a normal man.

In August 1987, Richard Seifried said he saw a Bigfoot

walk across a road at Crater Lake National Park in Oregon. "The exaggerated swing of [its] elbow seemed peculiar," he recalled in a written account. "[Its] quickness of step and gracefulness of stride pointed to only one explanation. Whatever it was, the furry monster was a new species.

"Unable to believe what I was seeing, I brushed my fingers before my eyes, trying to determine what was real. Yes, the creature was still there." Before Seifried could get a better look, the monster vanished into the shadows of the forest.

The next morning, Seifried met a female ranger who told him she'd had a strange experience during the night while sitting outside her cabin with her dog.

"A huge animal began smashing branches and logs along the creek bed," she told Seifried. "I'm not afraid of wild animals, but I was last night. And you know, my dog didn't pay the least bit of attention to those crashing sounds. Normally he would have been barking and trying to get loose."

The sounds the ranger had heard came from the same location where Seifried had seen Bigfoot. "The time of her experience was a mere half-hour after my sighting," recalled Seifried.

"Whatever it is, I—like a growing number of other people—know with certainty that [Bigfoot] does exist. We have seen it!"

Two years later, in 1989, Brenda Goldammer and her teenage stepson Nickolas encountered a Bigfoot outside their home in Yacolt, Washington. They heard a bizarre screeching in the nearby woods and stepped into the backyard to investigate. They were dumbfounded to see a seven-foot (2.1-m) tall, hairy, gorillalike creature. The beast turned and fled into the woods.

The following year, 1990, two separate groups of mushroom pickers on Mount Rainier, south of Seattle, reported hearing noises in the bush and smelling an awful odor. When they checked it out, they found huge footprints spaced two and a half times the average stride of a human.

Forest Service official Paul Freeman—who first encountered Bigfoot in 1982 in Washington's Blue Mountains—saw the creature twice more in the early 1990s. Ever since his first sighting, Freeman has been fascinated with Bigfoot and carries a video camera with him on trips into the wild.

In 1991 and again in 1992, Freeman identified strange tracks near Mill Creek as those belonging to a Bigfoot. He also found a strange handprint the size of a baseball mitt.

In April 1992, Freeman saw a Bigfoot for the second time in a clearing one hundred yards (90 m) away—and he captured the creature on videotape. Unfortunately, Freeman forgot to use the camera's zoom feature. As a result, details of the beast couldn't be seen on the tape.

Four months later, Freeman observed two similar creatures at Deduct Spring. He videotaped them from a distance. His tape—which some experts have called into question—has been shown on television several times.

Farmer Datus Perry, of Carson, Washington, has no doubts that Bigfoot exists. Perry says he has seen and heard the creature so often near his property that he doesn't pay any attention to it anymore. As proof, the farmer says he has an audio tape of a Bigfoot's roar.

Although most witnesses believe Bigfoot means no harm, there have been reported cases where the beast attacked humans—perhaps while defending itself.

In an article he wrote in the November 1995 issue of *Fate* magazine, Richard Seifried hints that a Bigfoot might have killed a person. Seifried talked to a member of a surveying crew who worked in a remote part of the Jim Bridger Wilderness Area of Wyoming several years ago.

"One night, as the survey team sat around their campfire, strange high-pitched cries alerted them to the fact that a large, unknown animal was also on the mountain," Seifried wrote. Although it was against the law to carry a gun in that area, one of the men had brought a disassembled 22-caliber rifle. He took it from his pack and put it together. Ignoring the protests of the others, he left the next morning to hunt for the creature.

After he failed to show up that night, they began a search for him the next day. "They found the rifle first," wrote Seifried. "It was lying alongside a trail, its barrel bent into a U shape. Next to the trail the land plunged into a deep canyon. At the base of the cliff they saw the lifeless form of their crew mate."

Cliff Crook, of Bothell, Washington, said he had a frightening experience with the creature on a camping trip near Duvall, Washington, in 1956. Crook and three teenage friends heard something in the woods. With their German shepherd by their side, they took a piece of burning log to light their way as they went to investigate. Suddenly they came face-to-face with a Bigfoot. The creature roared, picked up the barking dog, and threw it back at the boys as if the shepherd were a lightweight toy. Then the beast fled.

Virginia Swanson, a prospector who was working her ore claim in 1954 in the Big Sur area of California, recalled that she was camping one night when she was awakened by a powerful stench. She opened her eyes and at first thought she was having a nightmare—a Bigfoot had lifted Virginia and her cot right off the ground. The woman screamed so loud and long that the creature dropped her and ran off.

One of the most talked-about Bigfoot attacks occurred in

July, 1924, in the Mount St. Helens area of southwestern Washington. Two miners said they became scared when they heard eerie whistling and thumping sounds coming from a nearby ridge late at night. The noise, which continued every night for a week, seemed to be from an unidentified animal.

Eventually, the miners spotted a seven-foot (2.1-m) tall, apelike beast near the ridge. They were so spooked, they fired their guns at the creature but missed. Then they dashed to a cabin, where they thought they would be safe. But to their horror, they soon were surrounded by several more of the beasts. Throughout a long and scary night, the creatures threw rocks at the cabin and tried to smash open the door. The miners managed to withstand the terrifying attack. At daybreak the monsters grew weary and left.

When reporters for the *Portland Oregonian* heard about the assault, they visited the scene even though they had doubts about the miners' story. The reporters were surprised to find giant footprints around the cabin that headed off into the woods. (Ever since then, the spot where the incident occurred has been known as Ape Canyon.)

Is it possible that everyone who claims to have seen a Bigfoot is lying or mistaken?

Scientist Grover Krantz studied more than one thousand reports of sightings and interviewed dozens of eyewitnesses. He estimated that about half of them were "lying, were fooled by something else, . . . or gave me information too poor to evaluate. With the other half, I couldn't find anything wrong."

Even local governments don't deny the possibility that Bigfoot exists. Many have voted in laws that protect Bigfoot from being harmed.

Some believers think Bigfoot is a leftover from one of modern man's ancestors, known by its scientific name as *Gigantopithecus*. Numerous historical accounts from all over the world tell of wild, hairy men. However, western science does not recognize their existence.

Experts believe many so-called Bigfoot prints are hoaxes. However, tracks that aren't obvious fakes have been seen only in remote, seldom traveled areas, said James A. Hewkin of the Oregon Department of Fish and Wildlife. Many of the tracks are in regions of the Cascade Mountains that are nearly impossible to reach by people other than skilled hikers and climbers.

From his observations, Hewkin, a biologist, concluded that a "species of giant, bipedal primate [two-legged humanlike or apelike being], weighing up to eight hundred pounds [365 kg] and standing as tall as eight feet [2.4 m] . . . does, in fact, exist."

Deep footprints more than nine feet (2.7 m) apart allegedly made by a Bigfoot were closely examined in Grays Harbor County, Washington, an area of many Bigfoot sightings. The tracks indicated the creature stood more than seven feet (2.1 m) tall and weighed about six hundred pounds (275 kg). Hairs found at a site near Porter Creek were sent to the Arizona State Museum's Human Identification Laboratory. According to a published account, the hairs didn't resemble those of any known man or ape.

Despite the photographs, eyewitness accounts, and casts of tracks, scientists demand physical evidence—a skull, teeth, organs, or hair of a Bigfoot. Yet no bodies or skeletons of the creature have ever been found. However, hunters point out that they rarely find the remains of large animals because the bodies are eaten by other animals and scattered very quickly by scavengers.

Meanwhile, the search for Bigfoot continues. The question is: If these creatures do exist, how long can they stay hidden in the forests before we finally capture one?

47

LIZARD MAN

S eventeen-year-old Christopher Davis finished work at McDonald's shortly after midnight and hopped into his car for the long drive home on a muggy June night in 1988.

While listening to the music on the radio in his Toyota, Chris drove down a lonely stretch of road that runs along the edge of Scape Ore Swamp, four miles (6.4 km) south of Bishopville, South Carolina. He had driven this road many times late at night. But this would not be like any other night.

In the most remote part of the trip, his Toyota blew a tire. Grumbling about his bad luck, Chris pulled off onto the shoulder next to the smelly swamp. He got out his tools and a flashlight. Then, fighting off the mosquitoes, Chris changed the tire.

And that's when he experienced the scare of a lifetime—when he first sighted Lizard Man.

After tightening the last lug nut, Chris heard what sounded like an animal walking out of the swamp. At first he ignored it, but its footsteps grew louder as it came closer and closer to the teen. Beginning to get a little nervous, Chris gathered his tools and flashlight.

"I was putting the tools back in my trunk when I saw this thing with red eyes charging toward me," he recalled.

The "thing" was a creature that looked so unreal, Chris couldn't believe his eyes. According to the teen, the beam from his flashlight shined on a seven-foot (2.1-m) tall, reptilelike beast that forever would be known as Lizard Man. It had a green, scaly hide; hands and feet with fourteen-inch (36-cm) claws; a weirdly shaped, angular head; blazing red eyes; and a real problem with body odor and bad breath. Chris let out a yell, dropped his flashlight, and backed away.

"I ran to the car, got in, and just as I locked the door, the thing grabbed the handle," Chris recalled. "The thing was very angry."

Chris gunned the engine and the car squealed off. With his eyes glued to the road ahead, the terrified teen tried to catch his breath. He glanced down at his speedometer. It read forty miles (64 km) an hour. Chris assumed that by now he was far enough away from the monster to be safe. He was wrong. Suddenly he heard a mighty thump. It was Lizard Man. Chris hadn't realized that the creature had leaped onto the back of the Toyota before the car took off. The beast was now sprawled on top of the roof. Chris screamed in terror when he saw Lizard Man's moss-covered hand reach down and grab the windshield wipers. In a desperate attempt to get rid of the creature, Chris jerked his car from one side of the road to the other. The swerving worked. Lizard Man lost his grip on the car and fell off the roof. Chris then roared home.

The teen didn't sleep that night—or for several nights afterward. It all seemed so incredible. He wanted to tell others about the horrible incident, but he kept it to himself because he was convinced no one would believe him. Even he had a hard time accepting it. He probably never would have said a word to anyone had it not been for a married couple from Bishopville.

Three weeks after Chris's encounter with Lizard Man,

Tom and Mary Waye, of Bishopville, called the Lee County Sheriff's Department to report a bizarre happening. They said that their car was parked on the edge of the swamp when a reptilelike creature attacked it. The beast battered the chrome on their Ford LTD, ripped the molding, and scratched the finish. The couple said that the creature even stole their car's hood ornament.

At first, the police assumed it was a crank call. But when they went to investigate, they found the car had indeed been damaged. They still didn't believe that a monster from the swamp could have caused the vandalism.

When Chris Davis heard what had happened to the couple's car, he was stunned to learn that the incident occurred in nearly the identical spot where he had encountered Lizard Man. He knew then that he wasn't going crazy. So he called the sheriff's department to report that weeks earlier he had been attacked by the creature.

Soon the sheriff's office was getting flooded with calls from residents who swore that they too had seen Lizard Man.

One resident who lived near the swamp said that a huge beast with big eyes jumped out at him while he was getting water from a well. Another resident claimed he saw Lizard Man "big as anything, with glowing red eyes" standing by the caller's car.

Deputies heard from a man who told them that as he drove near the swamp, he spotted Lizard Man. According to the witness, the creature then chased after the petrified driver as he sped away. Incredibly, said the witness, Lizard Man managed to follow him for several miles—even though the car was going fifty miles (80 km) an hour.

A few days later, four teens reported that Lizard Man jumped in front of their car as it sped by the swamp. The driver slammed on the brakes and avoided hitting the creature.

Lizard Man stared menacingly at them before running off. He leaped over a six-foot (1.9-m) fence and disappeared into the darkness.

As more reports of Lizard Man came into the sheriff's office, so did calls from newspapers and radio stations—at the rate of three hundred a day. Some were from as far away as England and New Zealand, and all wanted news about the beast.

Radio station WSOC in Columbia, South Carolina, offered $1 million for Lizard Man's capture. "It's like Santa Claus," said Gerry McCracken, a spokesman for the radio station. "You know it isn't real, but in the back of your mind, maybe it is."

Callers to WSOC boldly promised they would bring Lizard Man in "damaged but alive," said McCracken "Those kind of guys are scary."

In the early evenings, residents were heading for the edge of Scape Ore Swamp, sitting in lawn chairs, hoping for a peek at Lizard Man. Others were prowling the swamp. The hope of that million-dollar reward shined in their eyes while the moonlight reflected off their shotguns.

Lizard Man–hunting tourists and story-seeking reporters continued to pour into Lee County. CBS News and *People* magazine interviewed the sheriff. *Good Morning, America* broadcast live from Browntown, an area near the swamp. CNN mentioned Lizard Man every hour for two days.

"I've talked with a number of merchants in town, and they estimate that about fifty thousand people came into the county in search of Lizard Man," said Sheriff Liston Truesdale.

Bishopville store owners were happy with all the visitors. The only place where business dropped off was at Lucius Elmore's butterbean shed, which was close to where Chris Davis met Lizard Man. People were scared to go there at first

51

because they feared that Lizard Man would attack them while they brought in their butterbeans to be shelled. Although no one ever reported being harmed by the monster, no one wanted to be the first.

Many people feared the creature, but others had a sense of humor about it.

Most of the stores along Bishopville's four-block business district sold T-shirts, bumper stickers, buttons, and caps that said, "Just when you thought it was safe to go into the swamp."

One lady called the sheriff's department and wanted to know if it was safe to let her children play outdoors. "Yeah," joked sheriff's official Billy Moore, "if you've got a couple to spare."

Despite Lizard Man sightings by responsible, levelheaded citizens, Sheriff Truesdale didn't believe in the creature. He thought there was a logical explanation. "I'm not saying that there isn't something out there, but I'm skeptical about the Lizard Man story," the sheriff told the *Lee County Observer.*

But then new evidence of a strange creature lurking around the Browntown area was discovered by a deputy sheriff and state trooper. They were responding to a report of a Lizard Man sighting near the swamp. Bizarre, three-toed tracks that measured about fourteen inches (36 cm) in length and seven inches (18 cm) in width were found on a dirt road. The prints were about one inch (2.5 cm) deep at the heel while the claws were about an inch and a half (3.8 cm) deep. The tracks continued for three hundred yards (275 m), finally disappearing into the swamp. Broken tree limbs and scattered trash were found next to the tracks.

The discovery brought out sheriff's investigators along with members of the State Law Enforcement Division and two bloodhounds. Officials scoured the area from four A.M.

until midnight, but they found no trace of man or beast. Plaster casts were made of the tracks and sent to the South Carolina Development of Wildlife and Marine Resources in Columbia for analysis. The identity of who made the tracks could not be determined.

A week later, new reports from witnesses indicated that Lizard Man was snooping around outside the swamp. A Lee County man told police that he had seen something "not human" running across a field near Elliott, South Carolina, about three miles (4.8 km) from the swamp. Three days later a woman called authorities, claiming that Lizard Man was standing outside her front door. But by the time the police arrived, the swamp beast had vanished.

Lizard Man was seen again—this time by a military man who previously had not believed in the monster.

According to Sheriff Truesdale, a colonel on active duty in the military reported spotting the beast. The colonel said he was driving along McDuffy Road when he saw a greenish-brown creature run across the road. It was about eight feet (2.4 m) tall with a tail that did not quite reach the ground, said the witness, who added, "It moved faster than any man I've ever seen."

The sheriff's office began an investigation but found no tracks because rain had washed them away.

"The witness wasn't a believer in the Lizard Man, but after this incident, he changed his mind," said the sheriff.

By fall, there were no more reported sightings of Lizard Man in the area. He has yet to make a reappearance.

Lee County, South Carolina, isn't the only place where giant lizardlike creatures have been reported. They also have been observed in Ohio and Indiana.

In 1955 a motorist returning home from work at three thirty A.M. near Loveland, Ohio, claimed he saw three weird creatures that looked like lizard men. He said they had wide, lipless, froglike mouths and wrinkles on their heads. As they walked along the Miami River, he watched them from his parked car for three minutes. Then he left to alert the Loveland police.

Three months later, Mrs. Darwin Johnson, of Evansville, Indiana, reported that she was swimming in the Ohio River when a clawlike hand gripped her leg from below the water and pulled her under. She struggled with a reptilelike creature and managed to free herself. But no sooner had she come to the surface than she was dragged down again. She was able to break free, and the attacker swam away.

Seventeen years later, in 1972, two Loveland, Ohio, police officers encountered a lizardlike creature. They said it stood four feet (1.2 m) tall on two legs, was frog-faced, and had a leathery skin. They saw it jump over a guardrail and run down an embankment leading to the Little Miami River. About two weeks later, one of the officers saw the beast again. The police officer shot at it, but missed.

To this day, no one knows what Lizard Man was or where he went. As Lee County Sheriff Liston Truesdale said, "Everybody likes a mystery—and this Lizard Man is a good one."

MOMO

A black, long-haired, manlike creature harassed farmers, fishermen, kids, and animals in the early 1970s in eastern Missouri.

The creature was known as Momo—named after the postal abbreviation for Missouri (MO) and the first two letters of the word "monster."

In the summer of 1971, farmers in Pike and Lincoln Counties, which are north of St. Louis, reported that their gardens and orchards unexplainably had been trampled. Their livestock had been startled and their dogs had howled. Some farmers said they had heard strange growls and weird screams in the night.

Authorities assumed a wild animal was to blame and did no follow-up investigation. At the time, they didn't know about the frightening incident that two teenage girls had experienced while they were on a picnic in a wooded area north of town.

On a July afternoon, the girls had parked their car and were placing their lunch on a picnic table when they smelled an awful stench. Suddenly, they later reported, a "half-ape and half-man" stepped out of a thicket. It walked toward them, making a "little gurgling sound." The horrified girls raced to their car and locked themselves in. But they couldn't drive away because they had left the car keys on the picnic table with their lunch.

"It walked upright on two feet, and its arms dangled way down," one of the girls told a reporter later. "The arms were partially covered with hair but the hands and palms were hairless. We had plenty of time to see this, because the thing came right over to the car and inspected it. This ape man actually tried to figure out how to open the doors."

The panic-stricken girls blew the car's horn. Apparently bothered by the noise, the creature backed away and ambled over to the picnic table where the girls' lunch had been laid out. The monster then ate a peanut-butter sandwich that belonged to one of the girls, before walking back into the woods. When they were sure it was gone, the girls grabbed the car keys off the picnic table and drove away.

They reported their scary encounter to the Missouri State Patrol. But the girls did not come forward publicly until a year later—after numerous other witnesses had claimed they saw the same creature.

"We'd have difficulty proving that the experience occurred," said one of the girls. "But all you have to do is go into those hills to realize that an army of those things could live there undetected."

Momo was given its name by the press in July 1972 when dozens of residents in and around the small town of Louisiana, Missouri, claimed they saw it.

Like the summer before, cattle and horses stampeded in the pastures for no apparent reason. Fruit was mysteriously stripped from the trees. Pumpkins, squashes, and melons were pulled from the vines. Police kept an eye out for anything suspicious but found nothing out of the ordinary.

However, private citizens did.

According to fishermen Johnnie Johnson and Pat Gorman, they were on the banks of the Cuivre River one night when they heard something splash a short distance upstream. Johnson's dog began to whine and cower in fear. Her tail was tucked between her legs, and her hair stood on end.

Johnson and Gorman then saw why the dog was so scared. A hairy, manlike creature had waded ashore and was climbing the steep bank less than one hundred yards (90 m) away from them. Both men were so shocked, they dropped their fishing rods. Hoping to get a better look, they raced to their pickup truck and turned on the headlights. But the monster had disappeared into the night.

"It looked like a large ape," recalled Johnson. "I've never seen anything in a zoo or circus that looked like that thing."

Frightened but curious, the two fishermen spent the next fifteen minutes driving slowly back and forth along the riverbank. Johnson shined his truck spotlight in all directions, hoping to catch a glimpse of the beast. They never saw it again.

They returned to their fishing spot and discovered that the creature had left tracks that were shapeless depressions in the sand. The men toyed with the idea of calling the police. But Gorman convinced Johnson not to report it because "people would think we were stark raving mad if we said we had seen a monster wade across the river and climb up the bank."

Nearby, early the next morning, a dairy farmer wondered why his three dogs were barking so frantically on the front porch. The dogs whined and howled because they wanted to come into the house, even though they knew they were not allowed inside. The farmer was puzzled because his dogs usually barked only when they were bringing the cows home.

When he opened the door to quiet the dogs, they nearly knocked him down as they rushed inside and trembled.

Outside, the farmer smelled an awful odor. Then he noticed an odd sight. A dark figure—looking like a large old man wearing a fur overcoat—was shuffling across a field toward the river about two hundred yards (183 m) away. Because the sun had yet to rise, the farmer couldn't make out exactly what he was seeing. But he knew this was no man.

"The creature looked like something partway between a great big man in a fur overcoat, a bear walking on its hind legs, and a gorillalike thing," the farmer later told the *Louisiana Press-Journal*.

The farmer ran inside and grabbed his rifle. Since the creature had trespassed on his property and frightened his dogs, he decided to scare it with a couple of warning shots. But by the time the farmer returned, the beast had left.

Later that morning, the farmer checked around the farm but failed to find any clues to the creature's identity. However, he did discover a strange set of tracks that led down to the river.

Like the two fishermen, the farmer didn't report the incident to police until the town learned of the bizarre encounters experienced by the Harrison family days later. The family lived at the base of Marzolf Hill, which lay near a large wooded area filled with caves and surrounded by farmland. The one-hundred-acre (40-hectare) area—home to poisonous snakes, bear, deer, and wild pigs—is roughly bordered by the Mississippi and Cuivre Rivers.

On the afternoon of June 11, 1972, eight-year-old Terry Harrison was playing alone in the backyard when he heard several deep growls. Terry turned around—and his eyes opened wide in terror. The growls, he later recalled, were coming from "a giant creature covered with shaggy black hair." Terry hollered and screamed as he dashed for the safety of his house.

When his fifteen-year-old sister, Doris, heard him yelling,

she looked out the bathroom window and gasped in astonishment. "About fifty feet [15.3 m] from the house I saw this big, hairy, black, seven-foot [2.1-m] tall beast," she told a reporter later. Doris said it was shuffling up Marzolf Hill behind their house and was carrying a dead animal under its arm. Meanwhile, the petrified children locked the doors and phoned their father, Edgar.

He rushed straight home from the café he owned in the town of Louisiana. Shaking in fear, his children told him what they had seen. Convinced they were telling the truth, Harrison ordered the kids to stay indoors. Then, armed with his rifle, he searched the hill.

Near the top of the hill, Harrison found an area of grass that had been trampled. It looked as if a large creature had been walking back and forth. Harrison noticed that most of the leaves had been pulled off a bush. He also noted that the area had a perfect view of his house below.

While examining the bush, Harrison heard a spine-tingling, deep-throated growl that echoed off the trees for several seconds. A piercing scream followed. Although hundreds of yards away, the shriek was still much too close for comfort. Harrison hurried down the hill to his house, where he phoned Louisiana police.

Chief Shelby Ward arrived with Gus Artus, a state conservation department wildlife official, and a reporter from the *Press-Journal*. After talking to the Harrisons, the three men were convinced that the family had had a terrifying experience.

After the Harrisons' story appeared on the front page of the paper the next day, hundreds of callers told police they had heard awful growls and loud, inhuman screams. At least a dozen reliable citizens insisted that they had seen a creature similar to the one described by Terry and Doris Harrison. The beast now had a name—Momo.

A few days later, at about one A.M., Edgar Harrison heard the creature crashing in the brush near his home. He and four other men searched the area throughout the night without success. The next evening, he again heard the beast running through the woods. This time Harrison led a search team of eight men.

The following night, at about nine thirty, the entire family "heard something that sounded like a loud growl," Harrison recalled. "It got louder and louder and kept coming closer. My family came running from the house. They jumped into the car and began urging me to drive off.

"I wanted to wait and see what it was that was making this noise. My family insisted that I drive away, and so I drove down the street. Over forty people were coming toward my house, some of them carrying guns. They had heard the same noise we did. I stopped the car and my wife told them: 'Here it comes!' And those forty people turned around and ran back down the street."

His family was so upset that they refused to remain in their house. Instead, they stayed at Harrison's snack-bar restaurant in town. Meanwhile, he continued to hunt for Momo on Marzolf Hill. But after being up for nearly six straight nights with very little sleep, Harrison gave up his search.

Others didn't. When Momo became big news, armed men poured into town, hoping to capture the creature. Hunters marched across fields and through gardens and orchards. Gates and fences were broken down. A bull, mistaken for Momo, was shot dead by a trigger-happy hunter.

To protect these people from themselves, Chief Ward placed a warning in the newspaper that no one with a gun would be allowed on Marzolf Hill. Violators would be arrested or fined. "We have no reason to think that the creature is dangerous," he told the newspaper.

Hoping to calm the residents near Marzolf Hill, Gus Artus told reporters, "Whatever the creature is, it runs from people. My advice is that people in that neighborhood should go inside their homes. If they are frightened, they should lock their doors. If something comes around their houses, they have plenty of time to call the police or a neighbor. They can also defend themselves from inside their houses, if necessary."

One of the reasons why the hunters failed to find Momo on the hill was because he apparently had moved to the banks of the Cuivre River.

Two men claimed they had been fishing in the river when they saw the creature wading across the water only about 150 feet (45 m) away from them. As soon as the beast spotted them, it began to run away. Meanwhile, the horrified fishermen dashed straight to the police station.

Chief Ward drove them back to the fishing spot. He noticed they had left in a hurry, because all of their fishing equipment was still lying on the bank.

They found three-toed tracks in the sand coming out of the river. The water was nearly six feet (1.9 m) deep at that spot, indicating that Momo had to be well over seven feet (2.1 m) tall.

Smaller but similar tracks were discovered a bit farther up the river. The second set of tracks was less than half the size of Momo's. Apparently the creature had a smaller child, mate, or companion.

Ellis Minor—a sixty-three-year-old woodsman, hunter, and fisherman—didn't believe in Momo. He thought it was a joke; that is, until he saw the monster himself.

Minor, who lived in a remote area near the Mississippi River, told the *Press-Journal* that he was sitting in his yard about ten thirty one dark night. His dog started growling and whining, so Minor turned on his flashlight to find out why. To his shock, Minor saw a manlike creature standing in the center of the road.

"It was no more than 125 yards [114 m] from me, and I had a good look," Minor recalled. "I couldn't see its eyes or its face, but it had coal-black hair nearly down to its chest. I'd guess it was pretty close to nine feet [2.7 m] tall and real broad across the shoulders. Everything about it was real big and scary."

As soon as Minor shined the flashlight on the beast, it turned and went back across the road and into the woods. A few minutes later, Minor heard the creature screech "like a woman would scream if someone attacked her on a dark night." He said it "made shivers run up and down my spine."

Minor told Chief Ward, "I'm not laughing at those Momo stories anymore. I've seen the thing myself, and it sure made a believer out of me."

About a week later, either Momo or one of its companions was spotted about fifty miles (80 km) south of town.

A Louisiana housewife, who declined to have her name revealed, told the *Press-Journal* that she had parked on a lonely road near Cuivre River State Park and walked into the woods to pick wildflowers. When she returned, Momo was standing just a few feet from her car. "I had always laughed at those monster stories," she told the paper. "But that thing was real, and I'm not kidding. I screamed so loud that they must have heard me in Booneville [about one hundred miles (160 km) away]. The monster loped off toward the river, and I ran for the car. I was shaking so bad though, that it took me about five minutes to unlock the door."

Strangely, Momo disappeared from the Louisiana, Missouri, area just as unexpectedly as it appeared. It has yet to return—at least, so far as anyone has reported.

THE JERSEY DEVIL

A mysterious monster that hides out in the remote woods and swamps of the New Jersey Pine Barrens has haunted south Jersey and eastern Pennsylvania, according to believers.

Although most experts declare that no such beast exists, thousands of people in thirty different towns claimed they saw the creature rampaging through the area during one astounding week in 1909. And ever since then, other witnesses through the years have sworn that they too have seen the monster known as the Jersey Devil.

According to James McCloy and Ray Miller, who wrote a book on the beast, "belief in the Jersey Devil is quite real, and [is] based on records going back through the years detailing concrete occurrences of this being. . . . The [Jersey] Devil's activities have been witnessed by reliable people, including police, government officials, postmasters, businessmen, and many others whose integrity is beyond question."

Descriptions of the creature vary, but supposedly it stands from four to six feet (1.2 to 1.9 m) tall. It has a head like a collie, the face of a horse, and a long neck. It flies with thin, two-foot (60-cm) wide wings. It has two short front legs with paws on them and longer but thinner back legs with horse's hooves. It utters an eerie cry that sounds like a cross between a screech and a wail.

Throughout the 1700s and 1800s, the Jersey Devil was thought of as nothing more than a scary myth. But all that changed during a wild, terrifying week in January 1909.

On the cold, snowy night of January 16, Officer James Sackville was walking his beat in Bristol, Pennsylvania. As he strolled across a bridge at about two A.M., he saw a creepy half-beast, half-bird. It let out a blood-chilling cry and hopped swiftly away. With his gun drawn, the startled police officer ran after the creature. When it raised its wings and took off, Sackville opened fire but failed to hit it.

E. W. Minster, the postmaster of Bristol, spotted the beast at about the same time. He told reporters later, "As I got up, I heard an eerie, almost supernatural sound from the direction of the river. . . . I looked out upon the Delaware and saw, flying diagonally across, what appeared to be a large crane, but which was emitting a glow like a firefly. . . .

"Again, it uttered its mournful and awful call—beginning very high and piercing and ending very low and hoarse. . . ."

In Burlington, New Jersey—directly across the Delaware River from Bristol—Joseph Lowden and his family reported on Monday morning that they had heard a bizarre noise during the night. "It was as if some heavy body was trampling in the snow of the yard," Lowden recalled. Whatever it was had circled the house and tried to get in through the back door before leaving. The family then found strange hoofed tracks in the snow leading to their garbage can. The contents had been half eaten.

From all over the city came sightings of an unearthly creature. Unexplained hoofprints in the snow were everywhere.

"Actual panic gripped Burlington that day," wrote

McCloy and Miller, authors of *The Jersey Devil*. "Doors and windows were barred and bolted in fear of possible attack, and many people refused to leave their houses, especially after dark.

"The tracks defied rational explanation. Hardly a backyard in Burlington was untouched by them. They seemed to climb trees, to skip from rooftop to rooftop, to lead into the street, only to vanish. They led across fields, over fences, into [hard-to-reach] places. They would appear for twenty yards [18 m] or so, and then completely disappear."

The weird hoofprints were discovered in several nearby towns that same day. An increasing number of people claimed they saw the winged beast. They called it "Jabberwock," "kangaroo horse," "flying death," "kingowing," "woozlebug," "flying horse," "cowbird," "monster," "flying hoof," and "prehistoric lizard," among other things.

In describing the creature, the local paper, the *Daily Republican*, said, "Hoofprints have been noticed in hundreds of places over a strip of country at least sixteen miles [25.6 km] long and three miles [4.8 km] wide.

"According to reports . . . [the Jersey Devil] jumps, flies, whistles, shrieks, squawks, gives forth [glowing] lights, and does all sorts of uncanny things."

One newspaper reporter in Bucks County, Pennsylvania, tried to form a posse to hunt down the beast. But he dropped the idea when no volunteers stepped forward. However, a similar hunt was organized nearby in New Jersey. Curiously, dogs refused to follow the creature's trail, turning away in fear. Hunters followed the tracks anyway for four miles (6.4 km), but then became frustrated when the trail suddenly ended.

Thirty miles (48 km) south of Burlington, in Gloucester City, New Jersey, Nelson Evans and his wife awoke in their home at two thirty A.M. Tuesday after hearing an unearthly noise outside. Peering out their bedroom window, they watched in frightful awe for a full ten minutes as the Jersey Devil danced on the roof of their shed.

Evans later told the *Philadelphia Public Ledger*, "It walked on its back legs and held up two short front legs with paws on them. It didn't use the front legs at all while we were watching. My wife and I were scared, I tell you, but I managed to open the window and say, 'Shoo!' and it turned around, barked at me, and flew away."

Wednesday, more men mustered up the courage to hunt for the Jersey Devil. A few of them said they actually saw it, but they got no more than a fleeting glimpse of it before it flew away unharmed.

Meanwhile, Mrs. Davis White told authorities she encountered the creature in her backyard in Philadelphia. Her screams alerted her husband, who dashed outside and chased the beast into the street, where it nearly was hit by a trolley car. That evening, forty miles (64 km) away, a police officer in Salem, New Jersey, spotted a large "devil bird" flying overhead. He shot at it but missed.

Several hours later, at one A.M. Thursday in Camden, New Jersey, about thirty-five miles (56 km) north of Salem, the Black Hawk Social Club was having a late meeting. According to member John Rouh, when he heard an "uncanny sound" at the back window, he turned to see the Jersey Devil staring back at him. Rouh screamed, and his fellow club members fled in terror. Rouh grabbed a big club to defend himself, but the creature took flight as it let out "bloodcurdling sounds."

About two A.M., passengers on a Camden trolley told police they saw the winged terror flying overhead, hissing loudly at them.

Trolleys in several towns now had armed drivers to ward off any possible attacks from the Jersey Devil. Businesses and schools closed as hysteria grew. Factories in Gloucester City shut down the night shifts because employees were afraid to go out after dark. Several theaters and restaurants in the area also closed because customers refused to leave their homes.

Local newspapers reported that many people who saw the Jersey Devil had fainted from fright. Mrs. Michael Ryan of Burlington reported that she froze from fear when she realized she was staring at the Jersey Devil. "For some minutes I was so frightened that I was unable to scream," she confessed.

Burlington Mayor C. Rue Taylor ordered police "to keep a sharp lookout for the creature and to shoot it on sight."

Meanwhile, the winged beast continued to harass people throughout south Jersey. Phone company lineman Theodore Hackett told the *Philadelphia Record* how he had rescued fellow worker Howard Campbell, who was chased by the Jersey Devil near Pleasantville, New Jersey, about fifty miles (80 km) southeast of Philadelphia:

"He [Campbell] became so frightened by the unusual appearance of the [creature] that he straightway made for the nearest telegraph pole. Letting out several yells for help and losing his wits entirely by the time he reached the top of the pole, Campbell threw himself out on the mass of wires between the two poles. [He] was lying there helpless by the time the rest of the gang, including myself, had arrived.

"Seeing the [Jersey Devil] on the pole, I raised my gun and fired. One shot broke a wing, and [the beast] fell to the ground, uttering hideous screams. But before anyone could collect his wits, the [creature] was up and off with long strides and a sort of hop, dragging one wing, and then disappearing into the pine thicket."

With ropes, said Hackett, they helped the shaken Campbell down from the wires. Luckily, Campbell was unharmed.

That evening, in the Camden suburb of Collingswood, the Jersey Devil perched on top of the roof of the fire chief's home. According to Alfred Heston, author of *Jersey Waggon Jaunts*, the firefighters arrived and blasted the creature with a spray of water from their hose. The beast ran down the street, but then turned around and charged toward its tormentors. Ignoring the sticks and stones the firefighters were throwing, the Jersey Devil bore down on them. Just as they started to duck and scream, the creature suddenly spread its wings, soared over them, and left the scene.

Later that night, Camden housewife Mary Sorbinsky ran out to the backyard when she heard her dog yelping in pain. She later told reporters that her beloved pet had been bitten by the Jersey Devil and was still in the "viselike grip of the horrible monster." Mrs. Sorbinsky grabbed a broom and whacked the creature until it let go of her dog. But then the winged beast flew directly at the woman before veering away at the last second. Mrs. Sorbinsky shrieked hysterically until neighbors rushed to her aid.

Moments later, the crowd, now numbering more than one hundred, spotted the creature screeching from atop a nearby hill. With the mob close behind, two police officers ran toward the hill and fired their revolvers at the beast, but it flew off.

Up to this time, the Jersey Devil had been regarded as a tall tale by those living outside the Pine Barrens. But now, major newspapers treated it as front-page news.

One report said that an expert from the Smithsonian Institution believed the creature lived in underground caverns and was a pterodactyl, a flying reptile that existed millions of years ago. Some people thought the beast was the result of an old Gypsy curse. Others worried that it came from another world.

Newspapers and zoos began offering rewards for the Jersey Devil's capture.

Philadelphia Zoo superintendent Robert Carson announced, "I don't know what animal it is, but if it is captured . . . the zoo will give a $10,000 reward. It will be a valuable addition to our collection. Undoubtedly it could draw crowds . . . and would be of educational value too—if it exists. But my private opinion is that it is going to be very hard to capture."

Many authorities thought that the Jersey Devil sightings were nothing more than a classic case of mass hysteria. One expert said the sightings were caused by "the mild but general idiocy on the part of the public."

Watson C. Buck, of Rancocas Woods, New Jersey, was a scared teenager when he encountered the beast during that week in 1909. On a local TV show in 1972, he told viewers:

"I'm over eighty, but I remember as if it was yesterday the night a mysterious creature appeared right outside my window. It was a cold, snowy night in the winter of 1909. I was sleeping in a little bungalow in Masonville.

"Suddenly something outside the place woke me up. The thing stopped at the window, and if I could only have pulled the curtain back I could have seen it. But I was too sleepy. The next morning I went outside and there they were—tracks in the snow at my window and all around the house."

When the TV interviewer asked him if they were the tracks of the Jersey Devil, Buck replied, "Who knows? I've done sixty years of research on the Jersey Devil, and all I can tell you is I just don't know."

After the wild week of sightings in 1909, the Jersey Devil

disappeared for a while. The only new tracks were those made by hoaxers. One con artist brought in a kangaroo, painted it with green stripes, and put fake wings on it. Gullible people paid twenty-five cents to see what he claimed was the Jersey Devil.

The monster went into hiding for several years before being spotted again in 1917. It was seen slinking through shadows around Valley Pond, New Jersey, in the winter, much to the terror of skaters. The creature showed up again in West Orange in 1928 before appearing in 1930 in Mays Landing.

Years later, Amanda Sutts recalled in a local newspaper her encounter with the beast on her family farm in Mays Landing: "We heard a scream near the barn one night and ran out of our house. The noise it made is what scared us. It sounded like a woman screaming in an awful lot of agony."

Mrs. Sutts said she not only heard the Jersey Devil scream many times, she often saw its tracks—all around the barn. She recalled that the prints were from eight to ten feet (2.4 to 3 m) apart and led to a large cedar swamp at the rear of the farm.

"When the horses heard the Jersey Devil scream, they would carry on so you'd think they were going to tear the barn down," she said. "You could hear it scream a long way off when the horses would quiet down.

"People may say there's nothing to the Jersey Devil, but I know darned well there is. Some might say I'm an old crank, but I know there is such a creature. I'll never forget how frightened I was when I saw it. I was so scared I thought I'd die."

In 1932 the Jersey Devil was chased by a posse in Downingtown, Pennsylvania. It escaped but left behind strange footprints that police said were "unusual in size." Three years later, it showed up again near Woodstown, New

Jersey. After reports that it had terrorized people, a group of farmers armed with shotguns scoured the surrounding woods in a futile attempt to capture the creature.

Sightings of the winged beast often have come before the outbreak of war. For example, it reportedly was seen in the Pine Barrens just before the beginning of World War I in 1914. People said they saw the Jersey Devil flying over the pines and dunes right before Italy invaded Ethiopia in 1937. Villagers of Mount Holly, New Jersey, claim the creature made an appearance over their town on December 7, 1941— the day Japan bombed Pearl Harbor, igniting the United States' entry into World War II.

Interest in the Jersey Devil dwindled until the 1950s, when reports of sightings hit the news again. Campers and motorists in the Pine Barrens claimed they heard the beast's shrieks. Some said they actually saw it in the woods or off by the side of the road.

In 1960 the Broadway Improvement Association of Camden offered a reward of $10,000 for the Jersey Devil— brought in alive. The merchants pledged to build a special zoo for the creature.

During the summer of 1963, the *Trenton Times* reported that five youths ventured into the Pine Barrens near Lake Atison in Burlington County in search of the Jersey Devil. They heard weird screaming after dark. "Like a pack of wild dogs," reported one boy. "Like the crazy screams of some cult worshippers," said another. They also found "large tracks in the underbrush eleven inches [27 cm] long."

In 1966 state police searched for a wild beast that had carried off thirty-one ducks, three geese, four cats, and two large dogs from a farm near a swamp in southern Burlington County. Near the farm, two troopers found strange footprints that were so large a man's hand couldn't cover them.

Over the next two years, the Jersey Devil was observed in Camden and Atlantic Counties, but efforts to capture it failed. A group of youths on a camping trip claimed they spotted it. One camper even tried to take its picture, but the photo showed little more than a gray blur.

Sportsman Edward Cornman of Ocean City established the Jersey Devil Association in 1969. He wanted to raise funds for a massive search to track down the beast that had been harassing south Jersey residents.

To those who laughed at his efforts, Cornman declared that no myth could survive this long "without there really being something out there somewhere."

Is the Jersey Devil just a legend? Or does such a creature actually exist? Wrote experts McCloy and Miller:

"Over the years, many have accepted the Jersey Devil's existence as fact. Others have derided and scoffed at it as baseless legend, and sometimes made those who believed in it objects of ridicule. But anyone who dares walk the lonely sand trails of the Pine Barrens or the mist-shrouded marshes of the Atlantic shore will find his eyes growing ever more alert, and feel just a suggestion of fear taking hold of him. It is hard to remain a skeptic alone in the curious New Jersey wilderness. An eerie presence moves there."

THE LAKE WORTH MONSTER

F or months during the summer of 1969, police in Fort Worth, Texas, received reports of a bizarre beast running through the brush at the Fort Worth Nature Center and Refuge.

Authorities assumed the creature was a prank. After all, the lake in the nature center was once the scene of a classic monster hoax in 1947. Back then a jokester had built a fake prehistoric water beast that he pulled with fishing line. Hundreds of people thought it was real.

But this latest creature—known as the Lake Worth Monster—was much different. Witnesses said it looked like a cross between a large man and a goat, weighed about three hundred pounds (135 kg), and stood seven feet (2.1 m) tall. It walked on its two hind legs and was covered from head to toe with whitish-gray fur. Some said it had small horns coming out of its head.

Police assumed that the monster was someone dressed up in a costume who was out to scare people. But authorities took the sightings more seriously after three badly shaken couples showed up at the police station early on the morning of July 10, 1969.

John Reichart told authorities that he, his wife, and two other couples had been parked at the edge of Lake Worth around midnight. Suddenly a huge creature leaped out of a tree and landed on the hood of the Reicharts' car. Before the shocked couples could do anything but scream in terror, the "half-man, half-goat" jumped off. Then it reached into the open window on the passenger's side and tried to grab Reichart's wife. Reichart managed to regain his senses in time and sped away before the monster could reach anyone.

They rushed straight to the police station to report the attack. Despite the couples' outrageous story, the officers believed the six had seen something truly astounding, because the witnesses were still trembling.

An investigator examined the Reicharts' car and noticed a deep eighteen-inch (46-cm) scratch running along the passenger-side door. Swearing that the gouge had not been there before, the Reicharts said it was caused by the monster's claws.

Returning to the scene with police, Reichart pointed out where the assault took place, but there was no sign of the beast.

"We made a strong investigation," Officer James McGee told the press at the time, "because those people were really scared. We've had reports about this thing for about two months, but we always laughed them off as pranks."

That afternoon, the *Fort Worth Star-Telegram* ran a front-page story headlined "Fishy Man-Goat Terrifies Couples Parked at Lake Worth." By nightfall the parking areas around Lake Worth were jammed with thrill-seekers hoping to meet what they now jokingly called the "manny-goat."

Late that night, the monster was spotted by a man as it crossed the only road leading into the nature center. The witness yelled at other people nearby to look. An estimated forty persons then watched in awe as the man-goat ran up and down a bluff.

Within a few minutes officers from the sheriff's department arrived on the scene and observed the strange sight. At first no one did anything but stand still as the

74

creature continued running back and forth several hundred yards away from everyone.

One of the witnesses was Jack Harris, of Fort Worth, who gave this account of that memorable night:

"We were driving around trying to find the monster. There were some sheriff's deputies asking us about it, and one of them was sort of laughing like he didn't believe it. But then that thing howled, and I think it stood the deputy's hair on end. He decided it wasn't so funny anymore.

"Those sheriff's men weren't any braver than we were—they ran to get in their car."

Harris said they heard the creature utter an unearthly yowl. But they still hadn't seen it. Suddenly, people heard someone yell that the beast was running across the road.

"I saw it come across the road, and I tried to take a picture of it, but the flash didn't go off," Harris recalled. "I took another picture but I didn't get anything because I was too busy rolling up my window.

"We watched the monster run up and down a bluff for a while, and other cars arrived. There must have been thirty or forty people watching it."

But then a few of the bolder onlookers decided to tease the creature. Armed with rocks and sticks that they planned to throw, they warily closed in on the beast. That's when the monster stopped running back and forth and flashed its anger at them.

"When some of them thought they would get mean with the thing, it got hold of a spare tire that had a rim on it," Harris recalled. "Then the creature threw it at our cars. The monster threw that wheel more than five hundred feet [153 m]. It was coming so fast that everybody took off and jumped back in their cars."

Another witness, Ronny Armstrong, said he was in his car when he saw the creature launch the tire. Armstrong was so scared that he threw his car in reverse and stepped on the gas. Unfortunately, he wasn't looking where he was going, and he backed his car into a tree.

Meanwhile, the beast escaped into the underbrush, but not before uttering a pitiful cry. "It was as if something was hurting the monster," recalled Harris. "But it sure didn't sound human."

Witnesses agreed that the creature walked like a very tall man but looked similar to a goat. They also were convinced this was no prank, because no one could fling a tire and rim five hundred feet (153 m).

Once again the creature made front-page news in a story headlined "Police, Residents Observe But Can't Identify 'Monster.'" The article featured a photograph of Armstrong with the tire and a dotted line showing the spot from where the creature had tossed it.

By now the Lake Worth Monster was receiving plenty of publicity on the radio and in the local papers.

"I'm not worried about the monster so much as all those people wandering around out there with guns," Sergeant A. J. Hudson told the newspaper. "Everyone rushed out there to hunt the monster, and a lot of them said they saw it looking [at them] in the dark."

Hundreds of Fort Worth residents armed with rifles and pistols headed for the nature center looking for the creature. "I'd guess that there are somewhere between two hundred and two hundred and fifty people out there beating the bushes," a police officer told the paper. "Most of them are inexperienced kids who will shoot at anything that moves."

After a teen was accidentally wounded by a trigger-happy monster hunter, police banned any guns in the area. So residents came armed with other weapons. "I've never seen so many knives, swords, tire tools, chains, clubs, and other weapons of every kind in one place in my life," Officer James McGee said at the time. "There's even one idiot out there with only a lasso. He says he's going to capture the thing, then sell it to the Forest Park Zoo for a million dollars."

In the following weeks, search parties made nightly hunts into the woods and fields along the lake. They found unexplained tracks—unfortunately not preserved—that reportedly were sixteen inches (41 cm) long and eight inches (20 cm) wide at the toes.

For a while it looked like the monster had been killed. One night, searchers who illegally had brought along rifles fired on the creature. They claimed that one of the bullets struck the monster, because it let out a squeal. They discovered a trail of blood and tracks, which they followed to the edge of the water. There were no more sightings for several days, leading people to believe the monster had died.

But then three men reported that the creature had leaped from a tree onto the roof of their passing car. The driver was so startled that he lost control of his vehicle and it slammed into a tree, throwing the monster off the roof. The beast then limped away. Although stunned by the experience, the three men were uninjured.

Shortly afterward, three searchers reported they had spent a week tracking the creature without ever seeing it. But they did hear its eerie cry at night. They also said they found several dead sheep with broken necks—victims, they believed, of the Lake Worth Monster.

Among the witnesses were at least two who snapped photographs of the creature. Unfortunately, neither picture showed much more than a gray blur.

Fort Worth housewife Sallie Ann Clarke, who claimed to have seen the monster four times, took one of the photos. When the story of the beast first broke, she assumed it was a big joke. Although the wilderness area around the lake is huge, she couldn't believe that a "manny-goat" could possibly live there; certainly not one that would make its home so close to a large city. On a whim, she drove out to the lake and found dozens of people looking for the beast.

Mrs. Clarke spent hours talking to them. Some claimed they had seen it. Several others swore that they had heard a piercing scream that could not have been human.

As she started to leave the area in her car, she saw a tall, gray-furred creature dart across the road and immediately disappear into the brush. Although she observed it for only a few seconds, she became absolutely convinced that she knew what it was. "I saw the Lake Worth Monster, and nobody can tell me otherwise," she declared. "That's the only thing it could possibly have been."

From then on, she spent night after night at the nature center, trudging through the brush armed with her camera, notepad, and tape recorder. She interviewed monster hunters and people who lived near the lake.

She also went through old newspaper files and archives and discovered that monsters weren't new to Texas. They had been seen there as early as the 1700s. According to several Native American legends, there had always been such creatures around Lake Worth.

Thinking there might be a connection between the beast and Bigfoot, Mrs. Clarke contacted John Green, Canada's foremost expert on Bigfoot. Green traveled to Texas and conducted his own investigation. Although he didn't know what the Lake Worth Monster was, Green knew it wasn't a Bigfoot. Both creatures were very large and walked on two legs, but the similarities ended there. "They're probably not even distant cousins," he told Mrs. Clarke.

Mrs. Clarke waited several months before getting what she

said was a photo of the monster. She was sitting on a tree stump when she heard hunters yell that they were chasing the monster toward her. She turned around to see the beast run past her. Mrs. Clarke jumped off the stump and snapped the photo as the creature rambled into the brush and disappeared.

But like other photographs of the creature, this one didn't reveal much. It showed the back of a gray, furry figure in the weeds taken at very close range. "I honestly don't think that the thing was more than ten yards [9 m] from me when I took the picture," she said.

By fall, there were only a few scattered sightings of the Lake Worth Monster.

The last person to file a report with the police about the creature in 1969 was Charles Buchanan. He claimed that on the night of November 7, he had been dozing inside his sleeping bag in the back of his pickup on the edge of the lake. Suddenly he awoke to discover that the monster was lifting him up. Buchanan grabbed a bag of the remains of a fried chicken dinner and threw it at the beast. The beast stuffed the bag into its mouth, plunged into the lake, and swam to a nearby island.

At the height of the monster scare, John Simons—a playwright who lived on the shore of the lake—couldn't bear the thought of someone killing or harming the creature. So he wrote a play called *The Lake Worth Monster* in the hopes that people would be more sensitive to the beast. The play was a local hit, performed before record crowds in Fort Worth.

"I feel sorry for the poor creature," he told the *Star-Telegram*. "It's lonely and it's isolated and it must be terribly afraid. I don't know for sure whether it's real or unreal—a freak or an apparition [ghost]. Anyway, that's not important. The point I want to make in my play is that the thing has not harmed anyone. It minds its own business. We should respect it—no matter what it is—and grant it the full protection of the law."

WHITEY

W here the White River runs beside the northeast Arkansas town of Newport, a large gray creature reportedly has made its home for the last sixty years.

The water monster first was spotted July 1, 1937. A farmer named Bramlett Bateman rushed into town, claiming he had seen a beast in the river "as big as a boxcar, like a slimy elephant without any legs." Bateman said he was walking alone along the banks of the White River when the creature suddenly surfaced. It was still thrashing about when the terrified farmer fled.

People hurried out to his farm south of town to get a look. Several respected citizens declared that they too had seen the monster—described as "a light-colored form slicing through the water"—before it sank under the muddy surface. Others reported seeing a tremendous disturbance in the river where water flew in all directions, and the waves rolled one hundred yards (90 m) upstream and downstream.

Nicknamed "Whitey" after the river in which it lived, the creature seemed to favor a bend that bordered part of Bateman's farm. The farmer decided to take advantage of the situation. He and the Newport Chamber of Commerce fenced in a viewing sight and then charged twenty-five cents for admission. Signs were put up along the roads for miles around that said, "This way to the White River Monster."

On July 15, 1937, the local newspaper, the *Jackson County Democrat,* reported that "hundreds of curious people journeyed to Bateman eddy [better known as Bateman's Bend], six miles [9.6 km] south of Newport, where several persons have reported seeing a gigantic monster in the stream. . . . Persons lined the shores in an effort to view the evasive creature. . . . [Two] residents reported it rose twice, after which they found masses of leaves floating down the river."

Journalists and curiosity-seekers from throughout the country flocked across Bateman's cotton and soybean fields that summer, hoping to sneak a peek at the monster.

But hardly anyone in the viewing area ever saw Whitey. Some people accused Bateman of making up the story of the beast so he could make money off the suckers who came to his farm. He flatly denied it. In fact, on September 22, 1937, he went to the county courthouse and made a sworn statement:

"I, Bramlett Bateman, state under oath that on or about the first of July, 1937, I was standing on the bank of White River about one o'clock and something appeared in the river about 375 feet [114 m] from where I was standing. . . . I did not see either head or tail, but it slowly rose to the surface and stayed in this position some five minutes. It did not move up or down the river at this particular time but afterward on many different occasions I have seen it move up and down the river, but I never have at any time been able to determine the full length or size of said monster. . . . There is no question in my mind whatever but that the monster remains in this stretch of river."

He said he could get sworn statements from at least thirty other respected citizens who declared they had seen Whitey.

Meanwhile, volunteers patrolled the riverbanks night and day. As the townsfolk became increasingly afraid to go into or near the water, officials thought about dynamiting the river to get rid of the beast. The town council chose instead to send a brave diver down into the river, hoping to find an answer to the creature's identity. He couldn't find any signs of Whitey. Apparently, the beast had moved downstream, and soon the number of sightings reported by the townspeople dropped.

However, Bateman claimed he observed the creature more than one hundred times throughout 1937 and 1938. But then Whitey seemed to disappear and everyone forgot about the beast—until the middle of June 1971, when the *Newport Daily Independent* broke a story that stunned the town.

One of Newport's most influential and respected citizens claimed he had seen a creature "the size of a boxcar thrashing around in the White River." The witness, who agreed to give his name to the reporter on the condition that it not be published, described the monster in vivid detail:

"I was on the shore, and suddenly the water began to boil up about two or three feet [.7 to 1 m] high. Then this huge form comes rolling up. It just kept coming and coming until I thought it would never end. I didn't see his head, but I didn't have to. His body was enough to scare me bad.

"It was smooth, gray, and long . . . very, very long. It didn't really have scales, but from where I was standing on the shore, about 150 feet [45 m] away, it looked as if the thing was peeling all over. But it was a smooth type of skin or flesh. . . . The thing was about the length of three or four pickup trucks, and at least two yards [1.9 m] across."

After the story appeared, local fisherman Ernest Denks stopped into the newspaper office. He said that he had seen the monster one evening a week earlier. But Denks hadn't said anything to anyone at that time out of fear that people would laugh at him.

"The thing I saw must have weighed at least one thousand

pounds [450 kg]," he told the paper. "It looked like something that came from the ocean. It was gray, real long, and had a long pointed bone [bulging] from its forehead. It was the darnedest-looking thing I've ever seen. When I saw it, I didn't hang around. I started the motor on my boat and got the heck out of there real fast."

Denks called the monster the Eater, because, he said, "it looked as if it could eat anything, anywhere, anytime."

About two weeks later, Whitey made another appearance in front of three astonished fishermen—including one who took a photograph of it.

On June 28, 1971, Cloyce Warren went fishing with two friends. Mooring their boat just south of the White River Bridge, they cast their lines. Suddenly the three men saw a huge column of water shoot up about two hundred feet [60 m] away from them. Taken completely by surprise, the men gaped in awe as a giant creature rose to the surface and splashed around before slipping under the water only a few seconds later.

"I didn't know what was happening," Warren told reporters later. "This giant form rose to the surface and began moving in the middle of the river, away from [us]. It was very long and gray colored. We had taken a little Polaroid Swinger camera with us to take pictures of the fish we caught. I grabbed the camera and managed to get a picture right before [the creature] submerged. It appeared to have a spiny backbone that stretched for thirty feet [9.1 m] or more. It was hard to make out exactly what the front portion looked like, but it was awfully large. It made no noise except for the violent splashing and large number of bubbles that surrounded it. I've never seen anything like what I saw."

The photo was published in the *Daily Independent,* but unfortunately it wasn't very good. The picture showed only a portion of what appeared to be a grayish creature sinking below the river's surface in a swirl of bubbles.

"My camera is only a cheap one, and I was shaking like a leaf when I took that picture," explained Warren. "I don't mind telling you that I was scared to death. That thing looked like something prehistoric."

Shortly afterward, another local fisherman, Lloyd Hamilton, claimed he snapped a photo of a "great, big, huge, spiny-backed monster." Hamilton took the film to the *Daily Independent* to be developed. But he forgot to mention that he had used color film. As a result, the negatives were developed as black and white, ruining the film.

A few weeks later, two local firefighters stopped into the office of Jackson County Sheriff Ralph Henderson. They told him they had beached their boat on Towhead Island—located on a lonely stretch of the White River south of town—and seen several strange, enormous tracks. Neither man could imagine what sort of creature could leave such bizarre prints in the sand.

Henderson and several other law-enforcement officers went out to investigate Towhead Island, which had a sandy beach stretching along one side of it. Brush, high grass, and a few trees covered the rest of the island. The river flowed slowly in this area and was over one hundred feet (30 m) deep.

The officers found the tracks without difficulty and stood staring in amazement. Each print was gigantic—fourteen inches (36 cm) long and eight inches (20 cm) across—and showed three toes with claws and large pads on the heel and toes. A distance of eight feet (2.4 m) stretched between each track. The sheriff estimated the tracks were about three weeks old—about the time fisherman Ernest Denks had spotted Whitey.

Sheriff Henderson said he didn't think the tracks were part of a hoax. "If someone faked these, he went to a heck of a lot of trouble and put them in a mighty unlikely place. Hardly anyone ever comes here."

While the sheriff and two deputies made plaster casts of the tracks, Game Warden Claude Foushee examined the rest of the island. At the upper end, he discovered another set of tracks that led to a grassy area close to the shore. The grass had been smashed flat as if something big and heavy had been lying on it.

The following month, fishermen Ollie Ritcherson and Joey Dupree reported they had a scary encounter with Whitey. They were in a boat on the White River between Bateman's Bend and Towhead Island—the area where Whitey had been sighted most frequently.

Their boat struck a large object that was just below the surface. Moments later, the object—which the fishermen determined was a monstrous creature—began to rise slowly. "Our boat was lifted completely out of the water and turned halfway around," recalled Ritcherson.

The fishermen never got a good look at the water beast, but they were convinced it was Whitey. After it lifted the boat, the creature slowly slipped below the surface, and the boat floated on the water.

"Whatever it was that came up under us was very large and very much alive," said Ritcherson. "I've fished that part of the river all my life, and I know every inch of it. There was no debris in sight, and you don't find tree stumps in water one hundred feet [30 m] deep."

Said Dupree, "It was no stump or log. We were just suddenly lifted up and turned sideways. We were both scared pretty bad, and we got the heck out of there as fast as we could."

Shortly afterward, Richard McClaughlin, of Lincoln, Nebraska, told Sheriff Henderson of an alarming experience he and his family had. The McClaughlins were enjoying a picnic lunch on the bank of the river (which happened to be a short distance away from the two fishermen's encounter). Suddenly they spotted a long, gray creature rising to the surface. It seemed to have a head and a spiny backbone.

"I'd estimate its length at between sixty and seventy feet [18.5 and 23 m]," said McClaughlin, "and I couldn't even begin to estimate how much it must have weighed." He said the monster thrashed around on the surface for nearly five minutes before sinking under the water.

When the sheriff told the witness it was probably the White River Monster, McClaughlin looked puzzled because he had never heard of such a creature.

Despite all the sightings during the summer of 1971, people weren't as fearful of Whitey as they were back in the 1930s. That may be because there were no reported cases of the beast ever deliberately attacking anyone.

By now, the national spotlight focused on Newport, a town of eight thousand. Film crews from CBS and Japan arrived to shoot the story of the latest sightings, while magazines, newspapers, and radio stations ran stories about the monster.

The state government decided that its famous river creature deserved protection. The Senate of the Sixty-ninth General Assembly of the State of Arkansas passed a resolution that: "The part of the White River in Arkansas from a southern point at Old Grand Glaise, Arkansas, to a northern point near Rosie, Arkansas, is the natural habitat of the White River Monster, and that this part of the White River be set aside and known henceforth as 'White River Monster Sanctuary and Reserve' and that it is unlawful to molest, kill, trample, or harm the White River Monster while in its native habitat."

Meanwhile, scientists from universities and even the

Smithsonian Institution came to Newport to learn more about the creature. But by the time the experts arrived, the Whitey sightings had stopped.

So what is—or was—Whitey?

Some people believe the beast is a dinosaur whose ancestors survived while most other species died out 65 million years ago. According to this theory, these dinosaurs live deep in underground rivers. But then in December of 1811 and January of 1812, a series of major earthquakes was centered in New Madrid, Missouri, about one hundred miles (160 km) from Newport. Perhaps, say believers, these earthquakes brought bizarre creatures such as Whitey up from the vast watery depths of underground rivers.

Others think Whitey is a little-known, whalelike animal that originally came from the ocean, because the White River flows into the Mississippi, which in turn drains into the Gulf of Mexico. Some scientists think it might be a giant fish—like a gar, sturgeon, or catfish—or a giant manatee (sea cow) or alligator. But people who have seen Whitey claim that theory is ridiculous.

Although the White River has an average depth of sixty feet (18.5 m) near Newport, it has deeper spots that could possibly hide a monster in its murky depths, say Whitey supporters. They point to the giant tracks on Towhead Island, Cloyce Warren's photograph, and the testimony of dozens of witnesses as proof that something very odd has been lurking in the White River.

Said local newspaper editor Mike Masterson, "It remains for some brave soul to venture forth to put a lasso (make that a chain) around the monster's allegedly adequate neck. When, and if, that time comes, the cries of hoax will vanish and the believers [in Whitey] can raise their chins in dignity, look the doubters directly in the eye, and say, 'See, we told you so.'"

THE FOUKE MONSTER

P eople in southwestern Arkansas swear that a tall, hairy beast who looked like a reject from a *Planet of the Apes* movie lived in the woods near the tiny town of Fouke.

The half-human, half-ape reportedly shattered the town's peaceful nights with an unnerving scream. The creature's noise caused frightened residents to lock their doors and grab their guns.

The Fouke Monster first gained attention in 1954, when the area was plagued by bizarre shrieks and wails coming from deep within the woods. The sounds were like nothing ever heard before. Armed searchers cautiously entered the forest looking for the source.

Late one afternoon, two men charged out of the woods, claiming they had just spotted a "large, hairy, manlike creature." The hunt continued, but searchers failed to find the monster. Eventually officials stopped looking, because the unearthly screams at night had ceased.

But then a few miles north of Fouke, a woman living with her small son and daughter saw a large hairy creature approach her house, according to the *Texarkana Gazette*. "She sent her son on a two-and-a-half-mile [4-km] run for help," said the account. "The boy, about seven years old, ran all the way to Fouke to tell the landlord to send help.

"'Go back and tell your mama not to worry,' he told the boy. 'I'll be down in the morning to see about you all.'

"Fearing for the safety of his mother and sister and probably scared out of his wits, the boy ran all the way back, arriving just before sundown. The creature had left the area, apparently returning to the woods as quietly as he had appeared."

Over the next few years, an occasional sighting of the beast filtered down to the police. But authorities assumed the beast was nothing more than a bear or mountain lion that had wandered from its normal territory.

However, in 1963 in the Jonesville Community, a few miles southwest of Fouke, several men claimed they spotted the monster. They said it looked like a seven-foot (2.1-m) human covered with brown hair. The men were so afraid that they shot at it. "We tried to get the dogs to [chase] the thing, but they wouldn't go into the woods," recalled resident Smokey Crabtree. "For three nights after that we used a wounded rabbit call and got the creature to answer, but the beast would never get close to us.

"It started making a noise like a house cat, then went into a chatter something like a goat, then like an owl. After a while it seemed to get annoyed and made a sound like a cross between a scream and a growl. That sound would really make your hair stand on end."

Most residents still didn't believe that a strange beast lived in their area. But they changed their thinking in 1971. That's when the Fouke Monster created havoc and quickly gained nationwide fame.

In late April that year, brothers Bobby and Don Ford and their wives Elizabeth and Patricia moved into a rented house near Fouke. They soon began hearing beastly screams in the night coming from a swampy, wooded area behind the house. One night, while the men were at work, the women heard strange footsteps on the porch. When they looked out the window, they saw an extremely large, tall figure turn and walk away.

The following night, when all four were asleep, the couples awoke to the sounds of stomping on the porch. The men took a shotgun and cautiously stepped outside. Because it was a moonless night, they couldn't see very well. However, they did observe a hulking figure as it stepped down from the porch. When it failed to heed their orders to halt, the men shot at it, but it escaped.

On the night of May 1, Elizabeth was lying on a couch in the living room when she noticed the curtain moving by the front window. "I saw a hand sticking through the window," she later told the *Gazette*. "At first I thought it was a bear's paw, but it didn't look like that. It had heavy hair all over it, and it had claws.

"I could see its eyes. They looked like coals of fire . . . real red. It didn't make any noise—except you could hear it breathing."

Elizabeth screamed, causing the other three members of the household to rush into the living room. They arrived just in time to see a large creature moving away from the window. The monster was black, hairy, and at least seven feet (2.1 m) tall with a three-foot (1-m) wide chest.

The men grabbed a gun and a flashlight and dashed outside. "At first I thought it was a bear," Bobby recalled. "But it ran upright and moved real fast."

Don shot at the beast several times before Bobby called Ernest Walraven, the constable in Fouke. He arrived shortly after midnight and examined the surrounding fields and woods for about an hour. Walraven told the *Gazette* that the creature matched the description of the one that had harassed residents of the Jonesville Community in 1963.

After searching the area around the Fords' residence, the constable gave them one of his shotguns and a stronger flashlight. Then he returned home. Meanwhile, the Ford brothers stood watch. "We waited on the porch and then saw the thing return and come closer to the house," Don recalled. "We shot again and thought we saw it fall."

But apparently it didn't fall, because the creature was not at the spot where they thought it should have been. Suddenly they heard the women in the house scream in terror. Bobby raced toward the back porch.

"I was getting up on the porch when the thing grabbed me," he told the *Gazette*. "I felt a hairy arm come over my shoulder, and the next thing I knew we were on the ground. The only thing I could think about was to get out of there. The thing was breathing real hard, and his eyes were about the size of a half-dollar and real red."

Bobby broke away and ran around to the front of the house. He was so petrified that he ran right into the unopened screen door.

"I've never seen anyone so scared," recalled his wife. "He was completely out of his head. Raving like a madman."

Walraven returned and stood guard while Elizabeth drove Bobby to St. Michael Hospital in nearby Texarkana, where he was treated for shock and scratches.

According to the *Gazette,* the next morning authorities found "several strange tracks that appeared to be left by something with three toes, and several scratch marks on the front porch that appeared to have been made by something with three claws." The tracks led to Boggy Creek, which flowed into a large swampy area known as the Sulphur River Bottoms a short distance from the house.

Police noticed that several pieces of tin, which had been nailed around the bottom of the house, had been ripped away. Also, another window was damaged.

The Fords refused to spend another night in the house. Meanwhile, Walraven met a neighbor of the Fords who said he had heard a strange howling noise during the night. "It came from the woods or the swamp," said the neighbor. "I couldn't tell which. It sounded like a woman screaming at the top of her voice, but I know it was some kind of animal."

As word of the monster spread, men carrying everything from knives to automatic weapons began searching through the woods and the Sulphur River Bottoms. Hundreds of sightseers flocked to the Fords' rented house. Sheriff's deputies kept running people off the property, warning them to stay away.

Meanwhile, Little Rock radio station KAAY offered a reward of more than $1,000 for the capture of the creature "alive and in good health." An official for the station said that because "the Fouke Monster has proven to be a source of mental anguish for the people of Arkansas, KAAY sees it as a public service to the state to do all it can to alleviate [ease] this problem."

Texarkana resident Raymond Scoggins offered an additional $200 for the live capture of the beast because, he told the press, "I want to preserve it in a zoo and discourage the killing of it."

Several teachers in the area begged residents not to shoot the creature and publicly asked the Arkansas legislature for help in protecting it. "The monster is a symbol of Arkansas's wild heritage," said a Pine Bluff teacher. "The state should appropriate [set aside] money for the capture and preservation of the beast."

By now more and more people reported observing the Fouke Monster.

On May 22, Mr. and Mrs. D. C. Wood, Jr., of Texarkana and their aunt Mrs. R. H. Sedgass said they were driving on Highway 71 south of Fouke about midnight when the headlights of their car shined on a huge manlike creature.

"I thought my eyes were playing tricks on me," recalled Mrs. Wood. "We were awed.

"It was hunched over and running upright. It had long, dark hair and looked real large. It was swinging its arms kind of like a monkey does."

Her husband said that when they first noticed the beast crossing the highway, he thought they were going to hit it. "It was really moving fast across the road—faster than a man," said Wood. "The thing didn't act like it even noticed us. It didn't look at the car. It seemed like a giant monkey in a way. It weighed well over two hundred pounds [90 kg]."

Said Mrs. Wood, "It was unbelievable what we saw. I had been reading about the thing, but I thought it was just a hoax. Now I know it's true."

Added Mrs. Sedgass, "I don't know what it was, but it was something big. Some people don't think there is anything to this monster, but I do."

A. L. Tipton and Robert Utke also claimed to have seen the monster the same night. "It looked like one of those things from that *Planet of the Apes* movie," said Utke, "except that this thing was a lot hairier."

Several nights later, three people in a Texarkana neighborhood spotted the monster squatting on an embankment across the street. "We shined a flashlight on the spot and saw the creature," Gloria Richey told the press. "He was real tall and hairy and had real red eyes. I thought the world was coming to an end. I have never seen anything like it. If you see it once, you never want to see anything like it again."

Added witness Junior Goodman, "When the light hit the creature, the dogs went wild. Then the monster started running through heavy brush, leaping over weeds, and running faster than a man could."

More than a dozen other residents reported that they saw the beast, and many more said they had heard it screaming.

Miller County Sheriff Leslie Greer, who organized an official search for the creature, found unusual footprints along the edge of Boggy Creek. Each print was about fourteen inches (36 cm) long and five inches (13 cm) wide, and had only three toes.

Identical tracks were discovered in a soybean field where farmer Yother Kennedy had been hearing bizarre animal screams during the previous nights. "I have never seen tracks like this, and I have been in the woods all my life," said Constable Walraven.

Frank Schambach, an anthropologist at Southern State College in Magnolia, studied a plaster cast of the footprint and declared, "It's not human, and I'd rule out any type of monkey or ape. All of them have five toes. Besides, there have never been monkeys native to North America, so that eliminates anything that could have been left over from times past."

By the end of 1971 there were no more reported sightings of the creature. Eventually, it was all but forgotten. Years later, the only reminder of the creature was a sign on the northern end of town that read: WELCOME TO FOUKE, HOME OF THE FOUKE MONSTER.

But then in 1991, the same—or a similar—beast was spotted again.

Two Oklahoma men, Jim Walls and his friend Charles Humbert, were traveling north on Highway 71 the morning of October 22. According to the men, as they approached the

Sulphur River Bridge around eight thirty A.M., they began to notice a strong, sickening odor. Fearing that a dead person was lying nearby, they stopped their pickup truck and looked along the side of the road.

Moments later, the men reported, they saw an eight-foot (2.4-m) tall, four-hundred-pound (180-kg) manlike creature covered in shaggy black hair running toward the south riverbank. The monster was upright and had a face that was more like a human's than a monkey's. The beast let out a piercing scream before it leaped from a thirty-foot (9-m) riverbank into the water, disappearing below the surface.

The sighting was one of four received by the sheriff's department that fall. But, as was the case twenty years earlier, authorities had no further proof of the existence of the Fouke Monster.

Even though the creature was sighted only in one small corner of Arkansas, it received more national exposure than any beast besides Bigfoot, thanks to Charles B. Pierce.

In 1972, Pierce, a Texarkana ad salesman, decided to make a film about the half-human creature. He convinced a local trucking-company owner to bankroll the project for $160,000. Then Pierce borrowed a camera that he barely knew how to work and assembled a cast and crew made up of local high-school and college kids.

He produced and directed a documentary about the Fouke Monster called *The Legend of Boggy Creek*. Although Hollywood studios would have nothing to do with it, the film became a big hit and earned nearly $20 million.

Pierce had made the Fouke Monster a national celebrity— one that apparently wanted no part of the civilized world.

VISIT PLANET TROLL

A super-sensational spot on the Internet
at http://www.troll.com

Check out Kids' T-Zone, a really cool place where you can...

- Play games!
- Win prizes!
- Speak your mind in the Voting Voice Box!
- Find out about the latest and greatest books and authors!
- Shop at BookWorld!
- Order books on-line!

And a UNIVERSE more of GREAT BIG FUN!

To order a free Internet trial with CompuServe's Internet access service, Sprynet, adults may call 1-888-947-2669. (For a limited time only.)